# The WildWatch Book

# THE WILDWATCH BOOK

Ideas, Activities, and Projects for Exploring Colorado's Front Range

Ann Cooper, Ann Armstrong, and Carol Kampert

Denver Museum of Natural History in Cooperation with Roberts Rinehart, Inc. Publishers

*For kids and their grown-up friends.*



Printed in the United States of America

Published by Roberts Rinehart, Inc. Publishers
Post Office Box 666 Niwot, Colorado 80544-0666

A Project in Cooperation with:

International Standard Book Number 0-911797-76-9
Library of Congress Catalog Card Number 90-81667

Design by Gail Kohler Opsahl
Cover illustration by Gail Kohler Opsahl

Production by J. Keith Abernathy, Kay Herndon, Danielle B. Okin, and Pat Werner
Illustrations by Ann W. Douden, Jill Haller, Marjorie C. Leggitt, and Gail Kohler Opsahl

# Contents

# Look for these symbols as you read:

[BEELINE]
Special places to wildwatch
(Numbers in parentheses refer to map and location guide in the chapter "More About Places to Explore.")

[CATERPILLAR]
Books to give you more detail

[LADYBUG]
Good news for wildlife

[FLYING LADYBUG]
Bad news for wildlife

[CHECK IT OUT]
Boxes to mark when you see the animals, plants, and wild clues mentioned

[COLORADO FLAG]
Colorado State Symbol

[BUTTERFLY]
WildWords you should know

# WildWatch Test

## Are You A WildWatcher?

Do you like beetles, bullfrogs, raccoons, and robins?
Do you try to find signs when the animals stay hidden?
Do you like tracks, bones, nests, cones, pods, snake holes, feathers, and all treasures of the wild world?

If you do, you're a wildwatcher!

**What counts as wildlife?**

■ Deer, ant lions, snakes, buttercups, and butterflies count as wildlife. They live without the care of people.

■ Cats, cows, canaries, and petunias *don't* count as wildlife. They need regular care from people.

**Where do you look for wildlife?**

■ Look anywhere and everywhere!

■ Wildlife is as close as your backyard, a vacant lot, or under a rotten plank in an alley.

■ Or go further to places such as Rocky Mountain National Park, that are kept natural. Animals and plants live there in truly wild settings, protected from the world of people.

**What makes the Front Range of Colorado special for wildwatching?**

■ Windswept plains,

■ tree-filled cities and towns,

■ open shrub and woodlands in the foothills,

■ dark, evergreen forests,

■ alpine tundra (on mountain tops, above the trees),

■ and having ALL these habitats (living spaces) close together! With such variety, many different plants and animals find places that suit them.

**Are you ready to wildwatch? Let's go!**

# WATCHING SKILLS

## Become a Better Watcher

The best way to see wildlife is to make sure wildlife doesn't see you first.

■ Wear drab—not brightly colored—clothes.

■ Keep perfectly still. Wait for animals to come to you. Don't follow or harass them.

■ Crouch down low to disguise your shape. Don't stand where you can be seen against the sky.

■ When you *do* move, move slowly and quietly.

■ Freeze if the animal you are watching looks your way.

Use all your senses to explore the world, just as animals do.

■ Look up, down, in, and under. Look big and look small.

■ Sniff out stinky skunks and musky foxes.

■ Listen for plopping frogs and mosquito musicians.

■ Touch test for slime, scales, stickers, or softness.

■ Taste is tricky. Some berries, leaves, roots, and fungi are edible. Some are deadly poisonous. NEVER taste unless a grown-up friend tells you it is safe.

# Tools of the Trade

Good eyes and ears are a wildwatcher's best tools. Fix a WILDPACK with other equipment, so you are always ready for an expedition.

**Here are some ideas:**

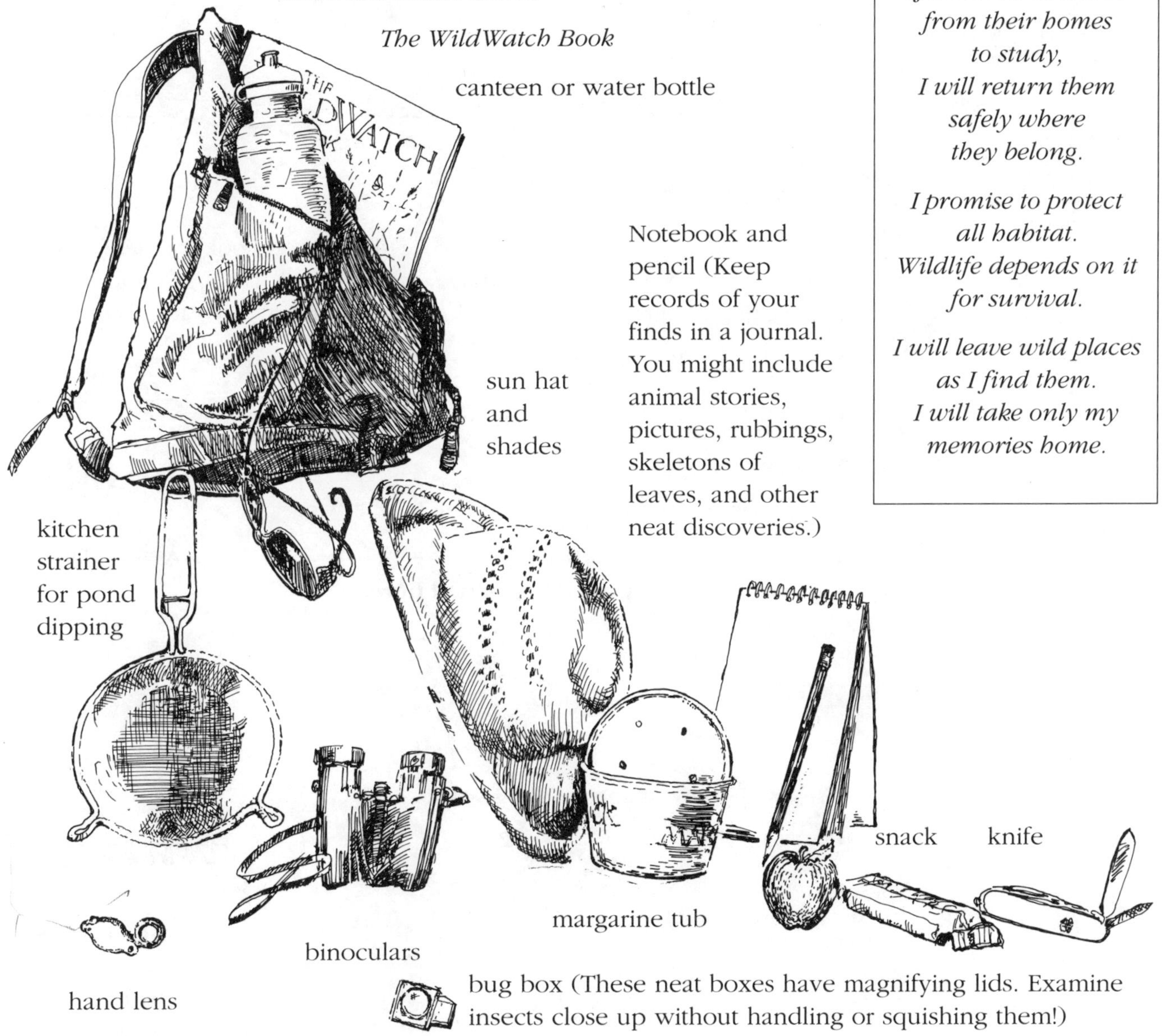

*The WildWatch Book*

canteen or water bottle

Notebook and pencil (Keep records of your finds in a journal. You might include animal stories, pictures, rubbings, skeletons of leaves, and other neat discoveries.)

sun hat and shades

kitchen strainer for pond dipping

snack

knife

margarine tub

binoculars

hand lens

bug box (These neat boxes have magnifying lids. Examine insects close up without handling or squishing them!)

Scientists don't know all the answers! You can be the first to discover new facts about plants and animals. Watch carefully. Figure out how the things you see help the animal or plant survive.

## Watcher's Promise

*I promise to respect all animals and plants. They have a right to live.*

*If I borrow animals from their homes to study, I will return them safely where they belong.*

*I promise to protect all habitat. Wildlife depends on it for survival.*

*I will leave wild places as I find them. I will take only my memories home.*

# WHO'S BEEN HERE?

Animals try to stay out of sight. If you walk in an area and don't see anything, DON'T GIVE UP! Be a nature detective. Look for clues and evidence. The signs will tell you who passed by.

## All Kinds of Prints

A print, or track, is the mark made by a single foot. Look for clear prints in snow or mud. A whole row of tracks makes a trail. Trails give more information about animal doings than a single print. They tell about:

1.

- the animal that made the trail,
- the gait (how fast the animal was going),
- the direction,
- and sometimes what happened along the way.

**Here are some to practice on.**
**Can you figure out what happened here?**

2.

*ANSWERS:*
*1. Squirrels are great acrobats. They can get to most feeders!*
*2. Looks as if the rabbit escaped from the fox this time!*

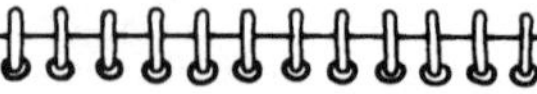

Next time you're out, try your skills at figuring out trail stories you see in the wild. Draw sketches of trail stories in your journal.

## Track Tester

What are *your* tracks like? Test them by walking across a newspaper with wet feet. Do all your toes show clearly? Which side of your foot presses the hardest? Does your whole foot show?

Different animals walk on different parts of their feet. People, bears, and raccoons walk on their whole foot. Dogs, cats, and coyotes walk on their toes. Deer walk on two toenails that have become hooves.

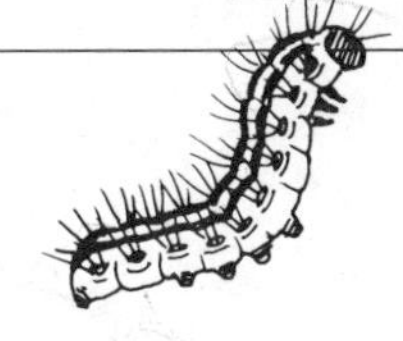

Want to read more about it?
*A Field Guide to Mammal Tracking in Western America.*
James Halfpenny.
For more information about tracks, trails, and neat animal signs.

## Potato Prints

(No, they're not prints made by a walking potato!)

**Make an animal print from a potato. You'll need:**

- a potato
- a magic marker
- a knife (ask a parent first) or a paper clip to dig and scrape curves
- an ink pad or some poster paint

Potato deer tracks

Practice drawing your print on newspaper first. Make it simple. You could copy a pet-print. Or choose something wild, or even imaginary, like bigfoot! Is your potato big enough?

Cut potato in half.

Draw print on potato with magic marker.

Cut or scrape away the potato surface leaving the print sticking up.

Press the potato on an ink pad or dip it into thick poster paint.

Then print!

Figure out the pattern of moving feet and make trails. Good for greeting cards, wrapping paper, secret signs, and whatever else you fancy.

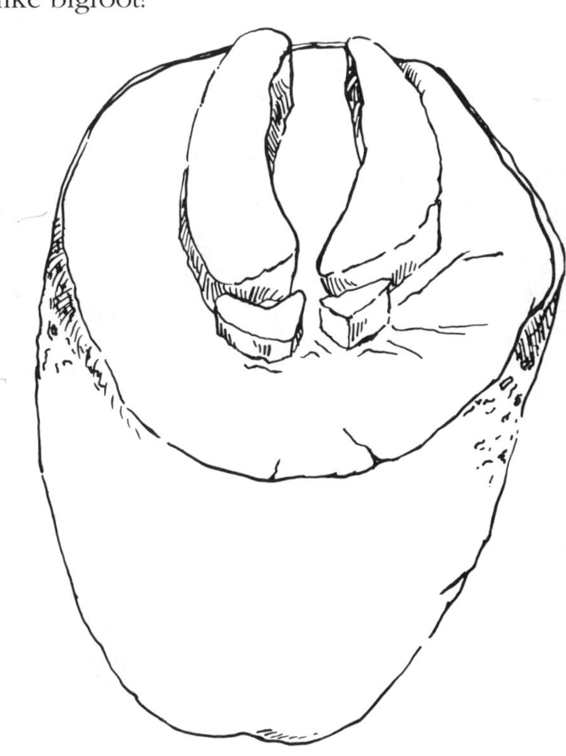

## Secret Pathways

Do you have a special route to walk to school or to a friend's house? Walking along a certain way can become a habit. It's the same for many animals. They travel the same pathways over and over again. Look for pathways and clues that tell who used them.

■ How wide are the paths? How high? Can you walk along them? Crawl along them? Or are they so tiny you have to explore them with your fingers? (Vole trails through grass are only about as wide as a bike tire.)

■ Do the paths go under fences? Is fur caught there?

■ Do paths go over fences? Look for deep prints where an animal might have jumped and landed.

■ Does the path smell? Use scent clues, too.

**Can you help the vole find its nest?**

## Munch Marks

Animals leave mealtime signs behind them when they move on. Look for these signs as you explore:

- ❏ Rabbits and voles leave tiny tooth marks on twigs.
- ❏ Beavers use felled trees for food and dam building.
- ❏ Look for caterpillars when you find chewed leaf-margins.
- ❏ Leaf miners eat leaves from the inside out, leaving skeletons.
- ❏ Porcupines leave bare yellow patches where they've eaten pine bark.
- ❏ Chickaree squirrels leave shredded cones in their middens (food mounds).
- ❏ Animal leftovers mark predators' dining tables.

Claw scratches mark boundary trees in a bear's territory.

**Carnivore:**
a meat-eater
**Herbivore:**
a plant-eater
**Omnivore:**
an everything-eater

## Magic Markers

■ Scraped and shaggy bark on a sapling show where a deer rubbed its antlers to mark territory or to get rid of itchy velvet in fall.

■ Rows of holes in tree bark are sapsucker signs.

■ Orange lichens on rocks may mark a marmot or pika lookout. Marmot and pika urine fertilizes lichens and helps them grow.

## Droppings Detective

Scat (animal droppings) tells about diet. Even if you don't see animals in a place, study scat to see which animal was there—and what they feasted on.

■ Scat with hair, bits of bone, or insect shells comes from a **carnivore**, such as a fox or coyote.

■ Scat with fibrous texture comes from an **herbivore**, such as a goose, deer, or rabbit.

■ Scat with berry stones and insect parts comes from an **omnivore**, such as a bear or raccoon.

## Pellet Clues

Owls feast quickly and silently in the night. A few gulps and their prey is swallowed up. But they can't digest fur, feathers, or bones. They cough them up as pellets.

The contents of pellets tell the menu. Who was dinner? A picked-apart pellet reveals small bones—skulls, jaws, leg bones, and shoulder blades.

Look for these "barf-balls," or pellets, under a favorite owl perch. (Check lookout trees on the edge of prairie dog towns. "Whitewash," or bird droppings, often marks an owl roost.)

NOTE FOR GROWNUPS:
If you are squeamish, owl pellets can be sterilized before your kids handle them by microwaving on high for 7 minutes, or baking at 300° for 30 minutes. It's a good idea to wash your hands after you've handled any animal material!

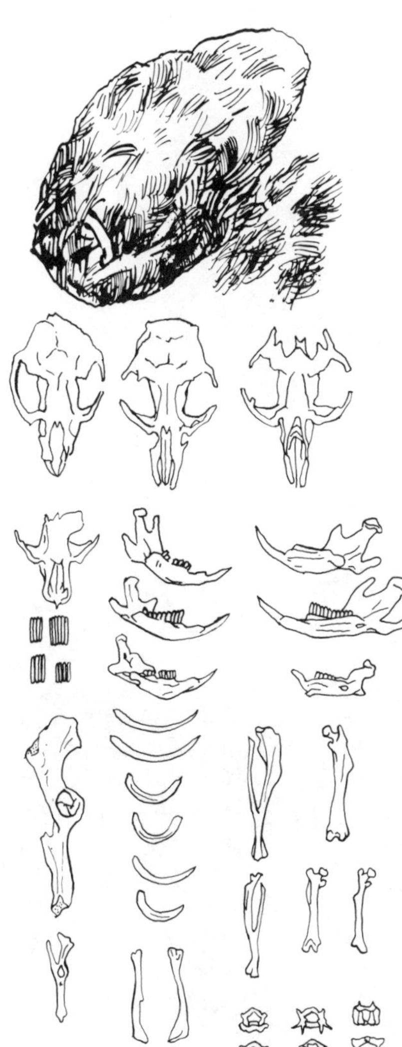

Inside an owl pellet

# Animal Actions

Sometimes animals behave in ways that are hard for people to understand. Ask yourself how the animal finds out about its world—by sight, sound, smell, taste, or touch? Ask yourself how the behavior might help the animal survive.

- Why does a robin tilt its head on one side when it feeds on a lawn?
- Why does a flicker drum on a metal power pole when there's no food in it?
- Why do bullsnakes flick their tongues out so often?

*ANSWERS:*
*1. A robin looks for worms with the down-side eye. The other eye watches for danger from above. The robin isn't listening for noisy worms!*
*2. The male flicker drums, "This is my place," as noisily as he can. He's claiming an area as his own and advertising for a mate.*
*3. Bullsnakes test air smells with their tongues.*

## Nifty Nests

Birds don't have to learn what kind of nests to build. They know by instinct. They get better at nest-building with practice. An experienced parent makes a neater nest.

Nests are often hard to find when they are occupied. The parent-birds select unobtrusive sites. Winter is a good time to search for nests. Bare trees are easier to check. And after a snowstorm nests may have snow hats!

See what nests you can spot. Who might have built them? Look at size, materials, and position.

How about building your own nest? Collect sticks to make a bowl shape. Line it with grass clippings or leaves. Would you make a good bird-parent?

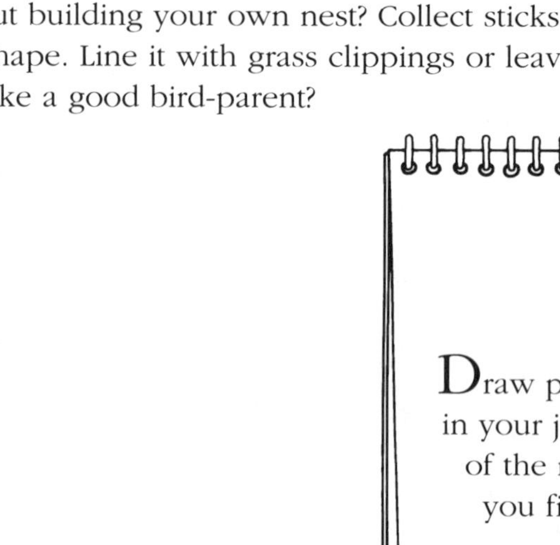

Draw pictures in your journal of the nests you find.

## For the Sake of Food

A home bird feeder is a good place to watch feeding behavior. (See page 30 for more about feeding birds.) Check the birds that eat at your feeder.

■ Do they have favorite seeds, fruit, or other goodies?

■ Do some birds glean spilled seeds from the ground?

■ Which kinds of birds are willing to eat together?

■ What makes birds leave the feeder?

■ Do birds of the same species share nicely, or do they squabble? If they squabble, does the same bird always win? (This is what is meant by the pecking order.)

Want to read more about it?

*Birds. A Guide to the Most Familiar American Birds.* Herbert S. Zim and Ira Gabrielson. For bird identification.

*A Field Guide to Nests, Eggs, and Nestlings of North American Birds.* Colin Harrison. For more about nests.

**Territory:**
an area defended by an animal to protect a home-site, food, or both of these

## My Home, My Munchies

Red-winged blackbirds need a place to live and hide. They need enough space to provide food for themselves and their young. This is their **territory.** Red-winged blackbirds set up territories around ponds and marshes. Watch there quietly to find answers to these questions.

- Do male and female blackbirds behave the same way?
- Which blackbird sings from high perches?
- Watch one male bird. Does he have favorite singing perches?
- What does he do if other male blackbirds come near?

Females are brown, with streaky camouflage.

Males are black, with red wing patches.

Need help figuring it out? Think about mother birds sitting tight on their eggs. Think about father birds keeping watch and sending intruders away.

Observe bighorn sheep in Rocky Mountain National Park (5) and near I-70 at Georgetown (18).

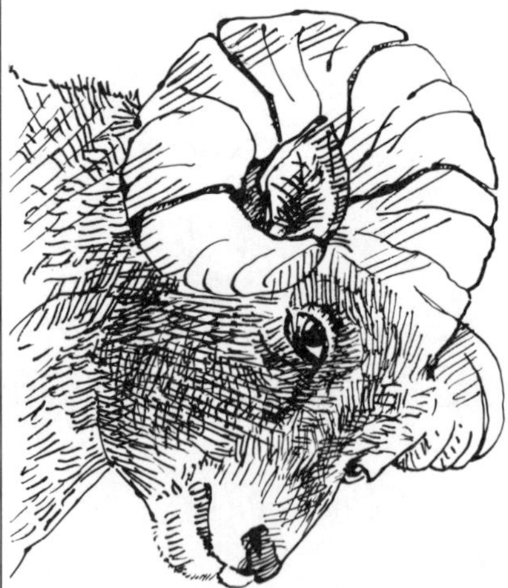

## Bighorn Behavior

Battling bighorn sheep clash their horns together. The crash echoes across the hillside. It sounds like a fight to the death.

It isn't! They fight to test which male is the strongest. That male will win the most mates. He'll father the most young. It is nature's way of making sure that strong lambs are born to carry on the species.

Both male and female bighorns have horns. They keep their horns for life. Horns keep on growing. They show a line for a year's growth, like tree rings. About how old is the bighorn in the picture?

Bighorn sheep is the Colorado State Mammal.

# Pooch-Person Dictionary

Many animals communicate with their voices. Another important way of "talking" is body language. Practice observing animal body language by watching a pet. Here's a pooch-person dictionary to help you translate.

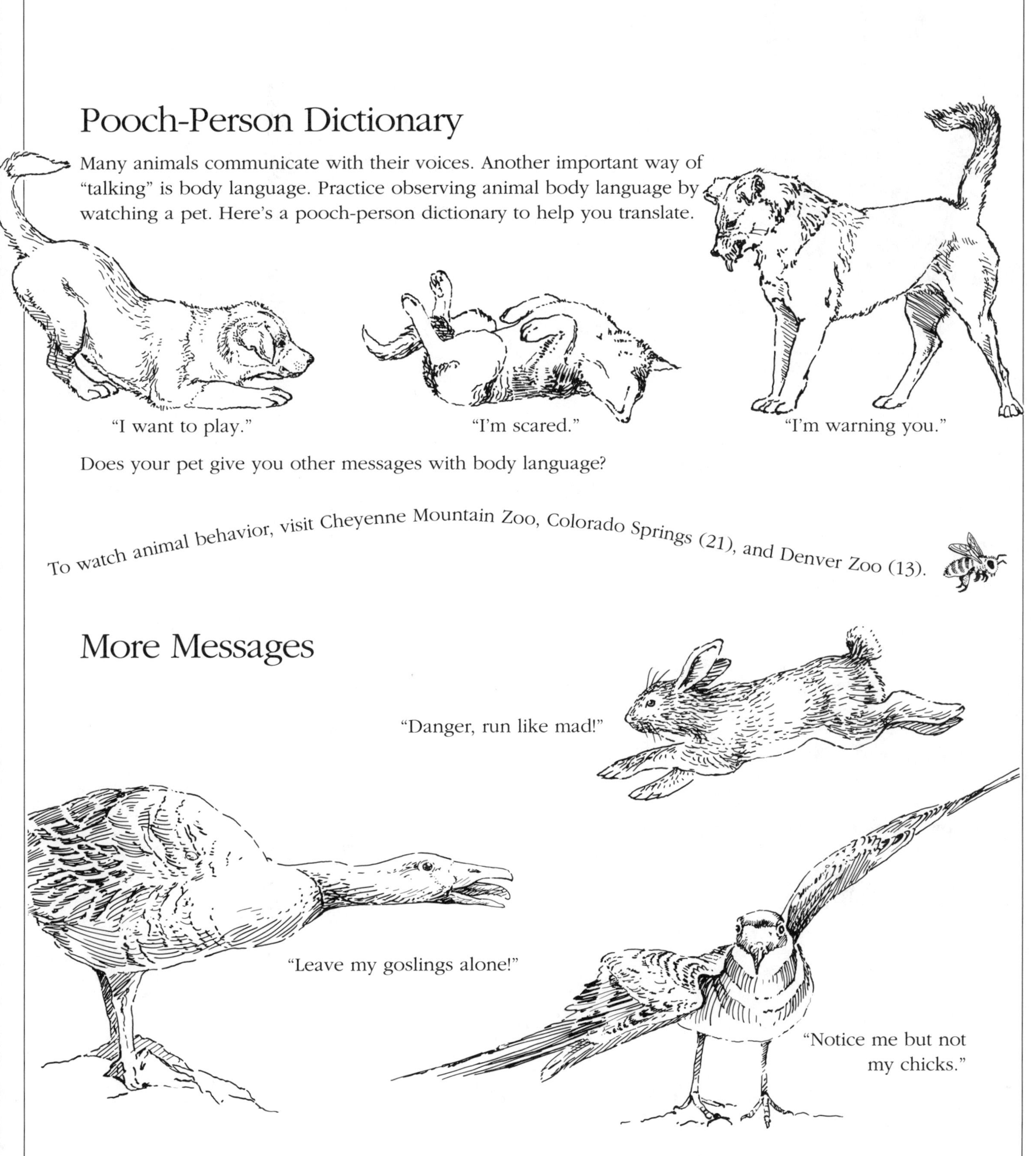

"I want to play."

"I'm scared."

"I'm warning you."

Does your pet give you other messages with body language?

To watch animal behavior, visit Cheyenne Mountain Zoo, Colorado Springs (21), and Denver Zoo (13).

# More Messages

"Danger, run like mad!"

"Leave my goslings alone!"

"Notice me but not my chicks."

# A Peek at the Past

## In Plain View

Dinosaurs, ancient mammals, and grasslands teaming with bison are part of our past in Colorado. Now, life along the Front Range has changed! People live everywhere. Towns, cities, super-highways, airports, shopping centers, and parking areas have split the land into pieces.

Close your eyes. Imagine the changes that have happened to the land where you are right now. What did this piece of land look like in the days of dinosaurs? In prehistoric times? 1000 years ago? When your grandparents were children? Today?

Observe Indian life at Denver Museum of Natural History (12). Visit the sod buildings at the Plains

Imagine you are the child of a Cheyenne family, or a settler family, and finally yourself again. What kind of shelter did you have? What did you eat? What did you wear? What did the land look like outside your home? What plants and animals lived there? How did you spend your time?

## Early Coloradans

Plains Indians made their living from the earth. Everything they needed came from the land—food, clothing, and shelter. They took enough for their needs. These were their only supplies for survival so they wasted very little. Above all else, they relied on buffalo (bison).

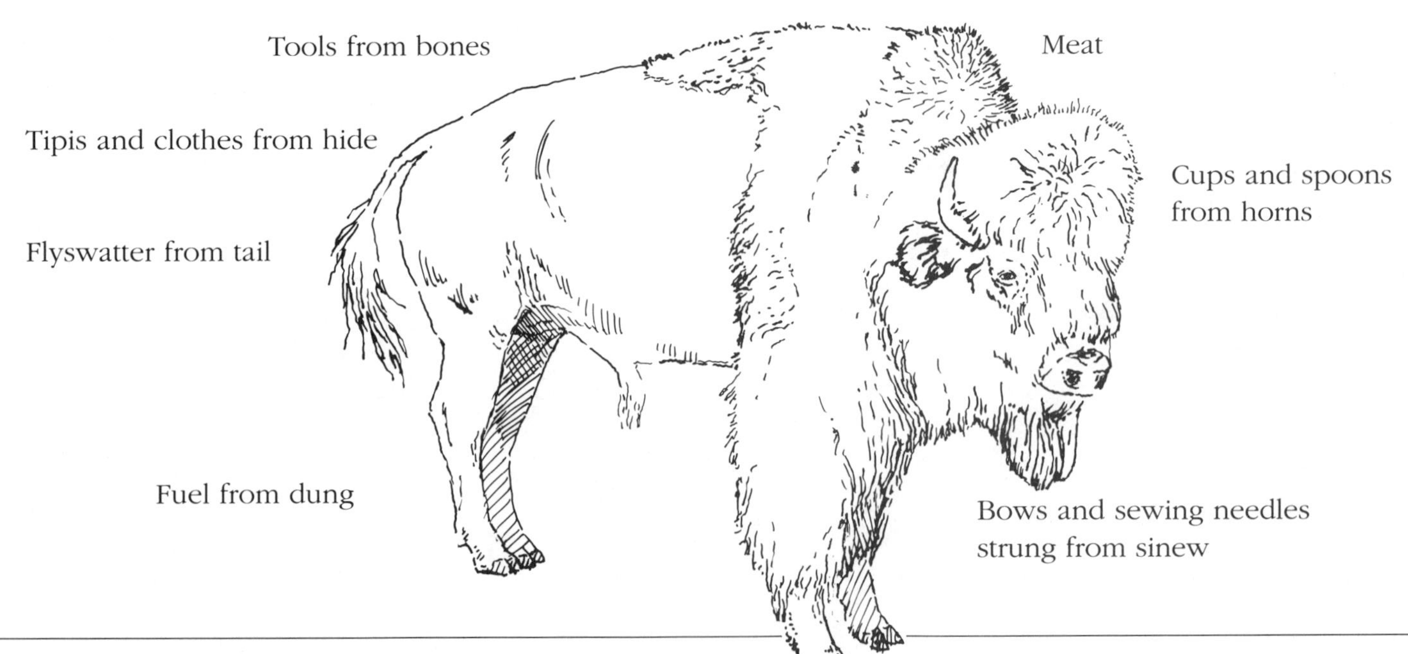

In your journal, draw Colorado as you imagine it was during the time of the Plains Indians, or before, when ancient mammals lived here.

Hunters with rifles came on the new railroads, shooting from the trains. They killed bison for food, for leather, and also for "sport." Later, settlers came and fenced the grasslands to keep in their livestock. The remaining bison could no longer move freely to other feeding areas.

The last wild bison in Colorado was killed at Lost Park, near South Park, in 1897. Present day bison live on preserves. Wild, free buffalo are gone from Colorado and so is the Plains Indians' way of living.

Conservation Center (15). Look for the bison herd at Genessee Park (16).

## Ancient Mammals

What was Colorado like when giant sloths, saber-toothed cats, woolly mammoths, and other ancient mammals lived here? Visit the Denver Museum of Natural History, or your library, to find answers to these wild questions.

- Were the Rocky Mountains here?
- Was the climate hot or cold?
- What did the animals eat?
- Were people around?

Woolly mammoths were **prehistoric** animals with shaggy fur and long tusks. They were relatives of modern elephants. They are **extinct.** A big pile of mammoth bones, along with some stone spearheads and big stones, was found at Dent, near Fort Collins, Colorado, when a flood washed away a river bank. How do you think these mammoths died?

Woolly mammoth

**Prehistoric:** a time before events were written down
**Extinct:** none left alive anywhere

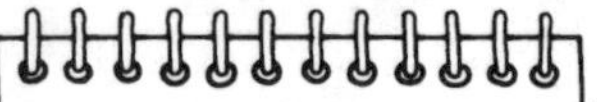

Find the answers to the questions below and then draw a picture in your journal of what you think Colorado was like in dinosaur days.

You can't zoom back to see how the Colorado Front Range used to be in the time of the dinosaurs. Instead, take a field trip to the Denver Museum of Natural History, or visit your library to find books about *Diplodocus, Stegosaurus,* and other animals of Colorado's past.

## Dinosaur Days

What was Colorado like when *Stegosaurus, Diplodocus, Tyrannosaurus,* and other dinosaurs lived here?

- Was the land flat or hilly?
- Was the climate hot or cold, wet or dry?
- Were there lakes, swamps, or oceans?
- What did the dinosaurs eat?

How do we know what the Front Range was like millions of years ago? We know from fossils. Most animals and plants rot away when they die. They are recycled back to the earth. A few dead animals and plants get buried in mud or in sandy and gravelly soils. Over time the soil changes to rock with the animal and plant remains preserved within it. These are fossils. Footprints, bones, skulls, teeth, eggs, shells, and impressions of plants can all be fossils.

1. Animal dies and is buried in silt.

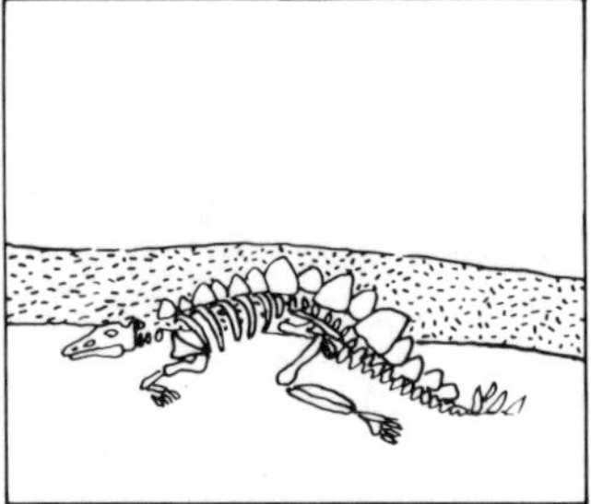

2. Over time soil changes to rock.

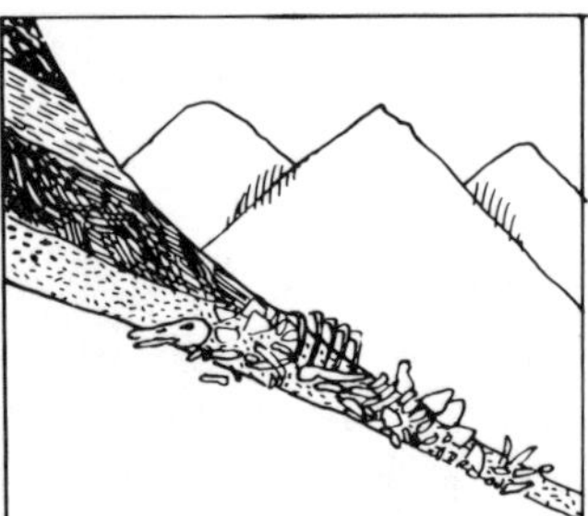

3. Fossil animals are exposed by erosion and weather.

Visit the dinosaur exhibits at Denver Museum of Natural History (12) and Dinosaur National Monument (1).

# Fake Fossils

**Make a "fossil" leaf print with potter's clay and a favorite leaf. You'll need:**

- potter's clay
- rolling pin or bottle
- leaf

Roll clay like cookie dough.

Make a clay/leaf/clay sandwich. Roll lightly to stick sandwich together.

Bake at 200° about 4 hours until dry.

Break apart your clay sandwich to find the leaf "fossil."

What has happened to your leaf?

**Make a "fossil" shell using plaster of Paris. You'll need:**

- plaster of Paris
- ruler
- pot for mixing
- plastic tub
- Vaseline®
- seashell
- water

Mix plaster with water until soupy. Pour 2 cm-thick layer into a plastic tub.

Coat both sides of seashell with Vaseline®. Press shell into plaster.

Cover with another layer of plaster.

Break apart the plaster when dry to find your fossil. Did you find a hollow with shell marks? Did you find a shell-shaped chunk of plaster?

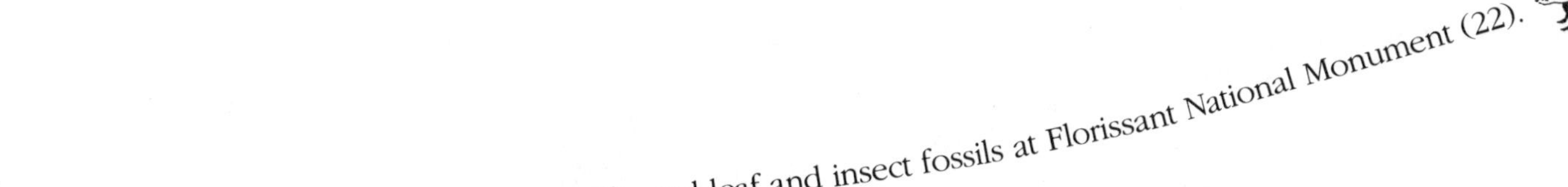

Suppose you found a fossil dinosaur skeleton. Could you guess what its body looked like when it was alive? What about its skin? Do you think dinosaurs were drab or colorful?

## *Stegosaurus* Statistics

**True (T) or False (F)?**

____*Stegosaurus* was a common dinosaur in the Front Range.

____ *Stegosaurus* is the Colorado State Fossil.

____ The first *Stegosaurus* skeleton was found at Morrison, west of Denver.

____ An adult *Stegosaurus* weighed as much as a large elephant and was as long as a school bus.

____ A *Stegosaurus* brain was the size and shape of a dill pickle.

*ANSWERS: They are ALL true.*

**Draw and color your own dinosaur around the *Stegosaurus* skeleton.**

The dinosaurs are extinct. Why did it happen? No one is sure. Here are some of the theories:

■ The dinosaurs died of a disease.

■ The climate changed gradually until it no longer suited dinosaurs.

■ Asteroids hit earth from outer space. They made a dust storm that stopped sunlight from reaching earth. The climate became too cold because of lack of sunlight and changed very quickly.

Or was it for some other reason? Scientists are still working to figure out dinosaur lives and dinosaur extinction. Dinosaur fossils are still being dug up in Colorado. They may help solve the puzzle.

Look at dinosaur tracks at Dinosaur Ridge near Morrison (19).

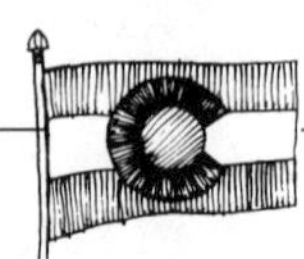

*Stegosaurus* is Colorado's State Fossil.

# COPING WITH CLIMATE

Our **climate** is the way it is because:

■ Colorado is far from any oceans. Our air is dry.

■ We are at high altitude, where air is thinner. Thin, dry air is a poor blanket. The sun warms us by day, but the heat escapes again at night.

■ Mountains to our west make a barrier. When storms move in from the west, we are in a *rain shadow*.

Colorado wildlife must cope with hot summers, cold winters, violent storms, and strong winds. It must cope with low humidity and big temperature changes between night and day. How can animals and plants do this—what **adaptations** do they have?

## The Snow Eater

*Chinook* is the Indian name for the strong, warm winds that blow down the mountains from the west. Chinook means "snow eater." These winds usually come in winter and quickly melt the snow. Air moves up the west side of the Rocky Mountains. It gets cooler as it rises. It drops its moisture as rain or snow. Then it rushes down the east side of the mountains, almost like a waterfall. It warms up as it pushes away the air that is already here.

## Snow and Wildlife

Some animals **migrate** to avoid the snows and cold of winter.

■ Broad-tailed hummingbirds fly south to seek nectar flowers and bugs.

■ Monarch butterflies flutter thousands of miles to sunny Mexico or California.

Some animals avoid winter snows by sleeping until spring!

■ Garter snakes **hibernate** with their buddies in holes underground.

■ Mourning cloak butterflies sleep in cracks in bark or in crevices of buildings. They'll fly on the first warm days of spring.

**Climate:**
the average weather of a place
**Adaptation:**
special feature that an animal or plant is born with that helps it survive in its habitat

**Migrate:**
move from one place to another, especially by the seasons
**Hibernate:**
sleep through the winter with the body thermostat turned down—slow heart, slow breathing, slow everything!

Do you have favorite summer animals that are not around in winter? Are they migrators or hibernators? Not sure? Find out at your library—a good winter project.

Some animals tough it out and keep going all winter! Extra-thick fur or extra-fluffy down feathers may help keep them warm. They need plenty of food to make body warmth. Travel can be hard!

## Snowshoes

Snowshoe hares live in mountain forests. In winter they feed on tree branches they can reach from snowbanks and on willow twigs and buds not buried in snow. How can they move over the deep snow without sinking? They hop along on the surface on furry, white snowshoe-feet!

## Wind and Wildlife

Wind can be a friend to wildlife.

■ It carries rabbit-smells to a hunting fox.

■ It floats spider-silk to an anchor place so the spider can make a web-framework.

■ It blows fluffy milkweed seed-parachutes to new places to grow.

Can you find other animals and plants who use the wind?

Wind can also be an enemy to wildlife.

■ It dries up delicate plants.
Look for plants with hairy leaves, waxy leaves, leaves with rolled edges, and very tiny leaves. These kinds of leaves resist drying by wind.

■ It breaks tree branches or blows down trees. Animal and bird homes crash down, too.

■ It blows topsoil away. Plants can't grow so well in thin soil.

Dandelion seed

Alpine forget-me-not

Keep a list in your journal of other plants or animals that are helped or hurt by wind.

## Rain and Wildlife

Gentle rain is a friend to wildlife, but heavy rain or hail can do great harm. Imagine the size of a hailstone compared with the size of an ant. It would be like us being hit on the head by a piano! All that water can't soak into the sunbaked earth quickly enough. It runs into channels and gullies and causes flash floods. How do animals protect themselves from heavy rain?

Butterflies use leaves as if they were umbrellas.

- Birds hide in dense bushes.
- Small mammals seek shelter in holes or nests.

Check out your animal neighbors in the next rainstorm.

## Sun and Wildlife

Here are some ways animals survive the heat of summer:

- Kangaroo rats stay cool in underground holes.
- Young great horned owls pant to keep cool.
- Mule deer feed at dawn and dusk and hide by day.
- Cold-blooded animals need the sun to warm their bodies.

Look for sunning snakes, toasting turtles, and basking butterflies. But even cold-blooded animals seek shelter when the sun gets too fierce. They disappear into holes, under rocks, or under shady vegetation.

Black-tailed jackrabbits have large ears that radiate body heat.

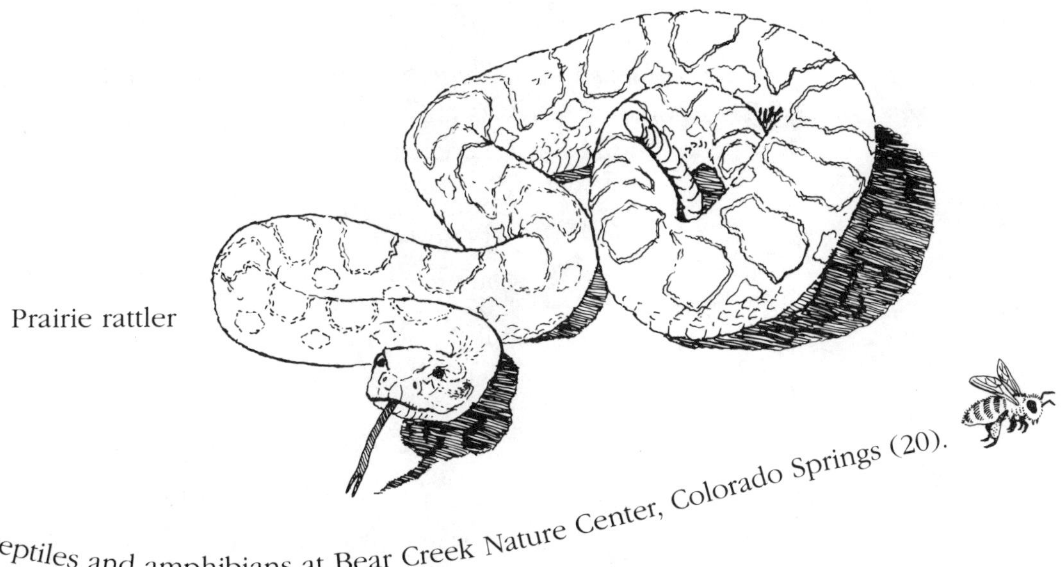

Prairie rattler

Observe reptiles and amphibians at Bear Creek Nature Center, Colorado Springs (20).

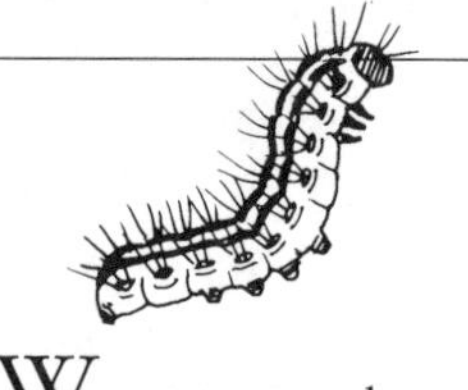

Want to read more about it? *Familiar Reptiles and Amphibians: North America.* John Behler. For good pictures of snakes, turtles, frogs, and more.

## Predicting the Weather

Long before weather satellites, radar, or weather balloons existed, people tried to forecast (predict) the weather using animal behavior. Some old-fashioned forecasts work. Others are just good stories.

**Can you judge these true (T) or false (F)?**

____ The wider the black bands on a woolly bear caterpillar, the colder the winter will be.

____ Swallows fly high,
Clear blue sky.
Swallows fly low,
Rain we shall know.

____ When squirrels lay in a big store of nuts, look for a hard winter.

*ANSWERS:*

*1. False. A nice story, but woolly bears can't predict bad winters.*

*2. True. Insects fly higher in good weather. The swallows follow them for a feast.*

*3. False. Squirrels store nuts every winter. They don't always remember where they put them! What happens to the nuts not found again?*

Chirp! Chirp!

## How Hot Is It?

Temperature is measured in degrees. If you don't have a thermometer try a Cricket Thermometer. Crickets chirp by rubbing their wings together. The warmer the air, the faster the cricket chirps.

Chirp!

Chirp!

Chirp!

Count the chirps in 14 seconds
Add 40
The answer is ___________ degrees F (Fahrenheit).

OR; Count the chirps in 1 minute
Divide by 5
Add 43
The answer is ___________degrees F.

Did you get the same answer both ways? Get metric! Figure the chirps in degrees C (Celsius). Celsius = (Fahrenheit degrees - 32) x 5/9

# City Settings

Wildlife that lives in the city has to put up with people! City plants and animals live with buildings, paved parking lots, and streets. They must adapt to the changes people make. What happened to wildlife that couldn't adapt? Those plants and animals were pushed out into wild places or died out. As wild habitat along the Front Range became smaller, less wildlife could survive there.

Just like animals in the wilderness, animals in the city need four things to survive: food, water, cover (hiding places), and a place to raise their families. They find these things in backyards, schoolyards, parks, alleys, golf courses, airports, and even inside buildings. Do you know other places, too?

People can design city green spaces to welcome animals. Look at HELPING HABITAT (page 27) for ideas.

## City Search

Is your part of the city a wildlife jungle? Go wild! Go hunting! Look up, down, around, under, inside—wildlife is everywhere.

**See if you can find these things:**

❑ A seed with wings. Can it fly?

❑ A crawly creature with more than ten legs. How many?

❑ A print in a sidewalk. Who walked there?

❑ A feather. What kind of a bird is it from?

❑ A spotted beetle. Where does it live?

❑ An animal picture or statue. What kind of animal is it?

❑ An animal home made of mud. What kind of animal lives there?

❑ A picture of our national bird. Where?

❑ Something worms would eat. What is it?

❑ A sow bug (roly-poly). Where does it live?

Leave living things in their homes! Draw pictures, or write about what you see in your journal.

# Map a Green Space

Choose a green space near your home. It could be your yard. It could be a park.

**Draw a map showing trees, shrubs, and grassy areas. Mark in people-pathways.**

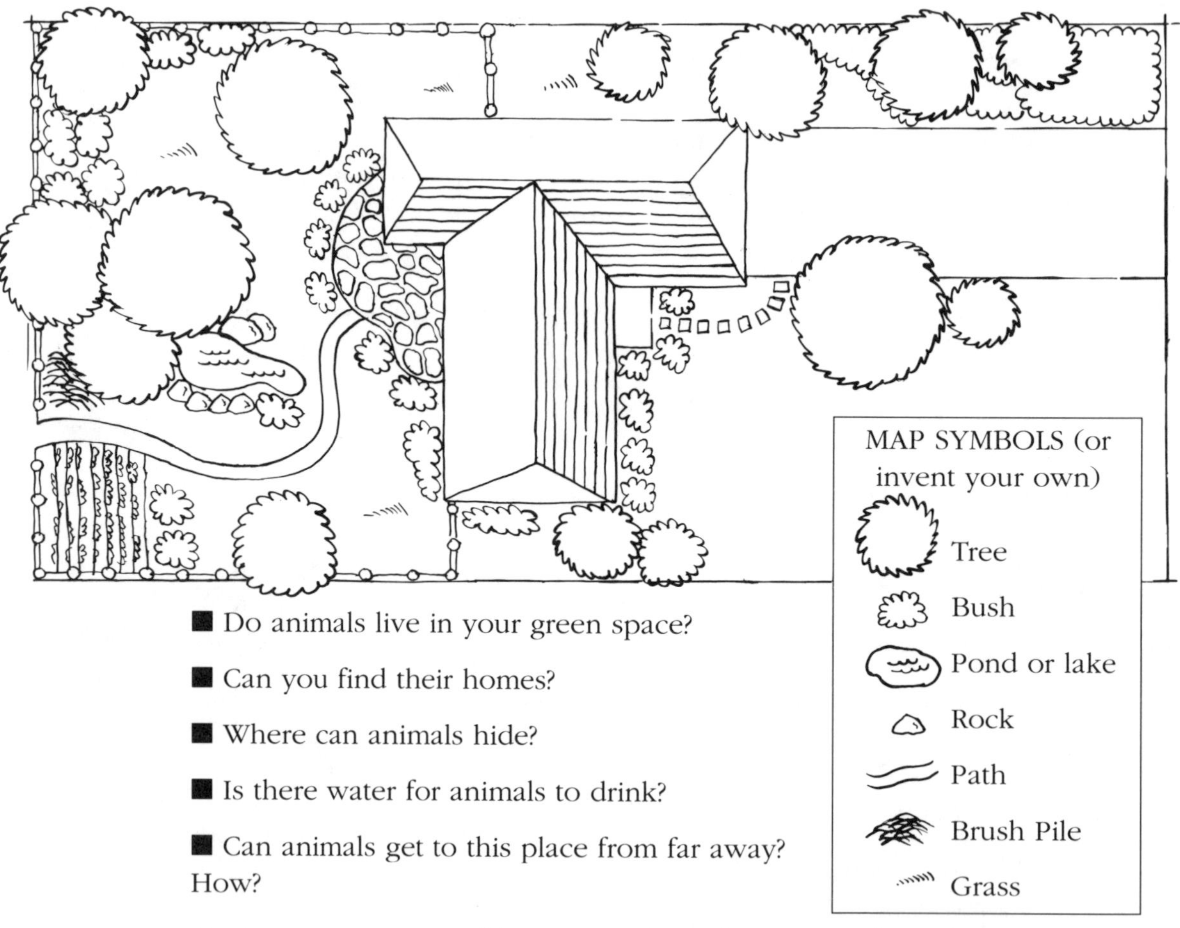


■ Do animals live in your green space?

■ Can you find their homes?

■ Where can animals hide?

■ Is there water for animals to drink?

■ Can animals get to this place from far away? How?

Most green spaces are like islands. Animals can't get from one green island to another without risking danger from people, traffic, and highways.

That's fine for small animals. They find all they need in one green island. They live their entire lives there. Larger animals must invent ways to get from one island to another safely. One island can't fill their need for food, water, cover, and a home. Pronghorn, elk, and mountain lions need bigger spaces than a city can provide. They live in wild places and usually avoid cities.

## Animal Interstates?

■ Rivers are natural travel routes for animals. Tree tangles give cover.

■ Irrigation ditches make good wild corridors if they are not tidy, polluted, or made of concrete.

■ Overhead wires give squirrels tightrope walkways that can keep them from traffic danger.

■ Sewers and drainage pipes act as raccoon subways.

## Raccoon Tales

The name *raccoon* comes from the Algonquin Indian word *arakunem.* It means, "He who scratches with his hands." In wild places raccoons make dens in hollow trees. Babies are born in the dens. But raccoons also have figured out how to live with people. City raccoons can't all find hollow trees. Some use sewer pipes, culverts, and drains as homes. Some live in style in chimneys and attics. City raccoons dine on people's leftovers. Watch out for a shadowy shape disappearing in the night. It could be a hunting raccoon.

**Which of these foods will raccoons eat? Circle them!**

| | | |
|---|---|---|
| goldfish | sweet corn | dog chow |
| garbage | berries | bones |
| worms | mushrooms | tomatoes |
| popcorn | grapes | mice |

*ANSWER: Raccoons are omnivorous. They eat all these foods, although they don't seem to like tomatoes very much!*

■ Do raccoons wash their food?

■ Are they fussy, clean animals?

■ Do they wet their food because they don't have enough spit to swallow dry food?

*ANSWERS: No way! Although raccoons do dunk food if there is water handy, it isn't really washing. Raccoons will eat food that is dirty. They'll dunk food that is clean. If there is no water nearby, raccoons will gobble up a dry and dirty meal. They have plenty of saliva (spit) to digest the food. Why, then, do they dunk their food? Nobody knows for sure!*

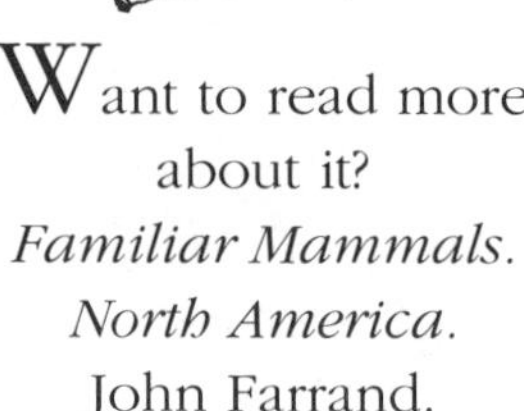

Want to read more about it? *Familiar Mammals. North America.* John Farrand.

# Foxy Squirrels

Fox squirrels are at home in the city. They like the big trees in our parks and gardens. They didn't always live in Colorado. They are easterners. But as people planted trees in towns and cities, life along the Front Range began to suit them. Solve these puzzles by watching fox squirrels in your neighborhood.

- What kind of homes do they build?
- What do they eat, and what do they do with extra food?
- What noise do they make when they're scared?
- How much time do they spend on the ground?
- Do they nap? Where?
- What do they use their tails for?

# Three Cheers for Trees

Trees are good air conditioners. They breathe out water through tiny holes (stomates) in their leaves. When water turns to vapor, it takes heat away with it (the same way you cool off quickly when your skin is wet). That's why trees make cool, shady hideouts on hot days.

Trees clean the city air. They take in carbon dioxide, which builds up from car exhausts and factory chimneys. They give off oxygen that animals and people need to breathe.

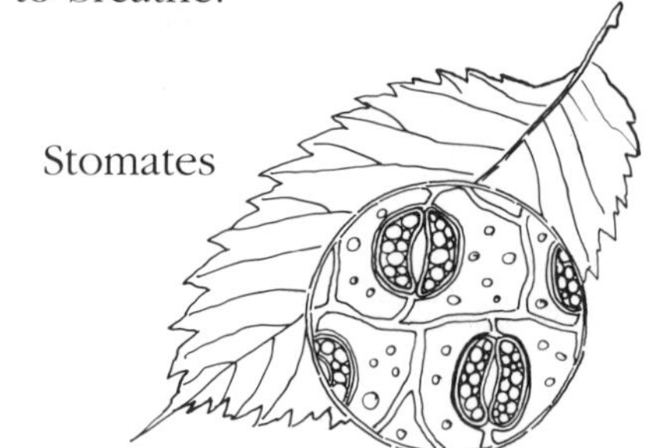


Take a tree walk in the City Park, Fort Collins (3).

A wildlife smile to all tree planters! Does your school do something special for Arbor Day? If not, then why don't you and your friends start a project? (In Colorado, Arbor Day is celebrated on the third Friday in April.)

## House Hunting

**Check out the local real estate. Try to match a home with its owner.**

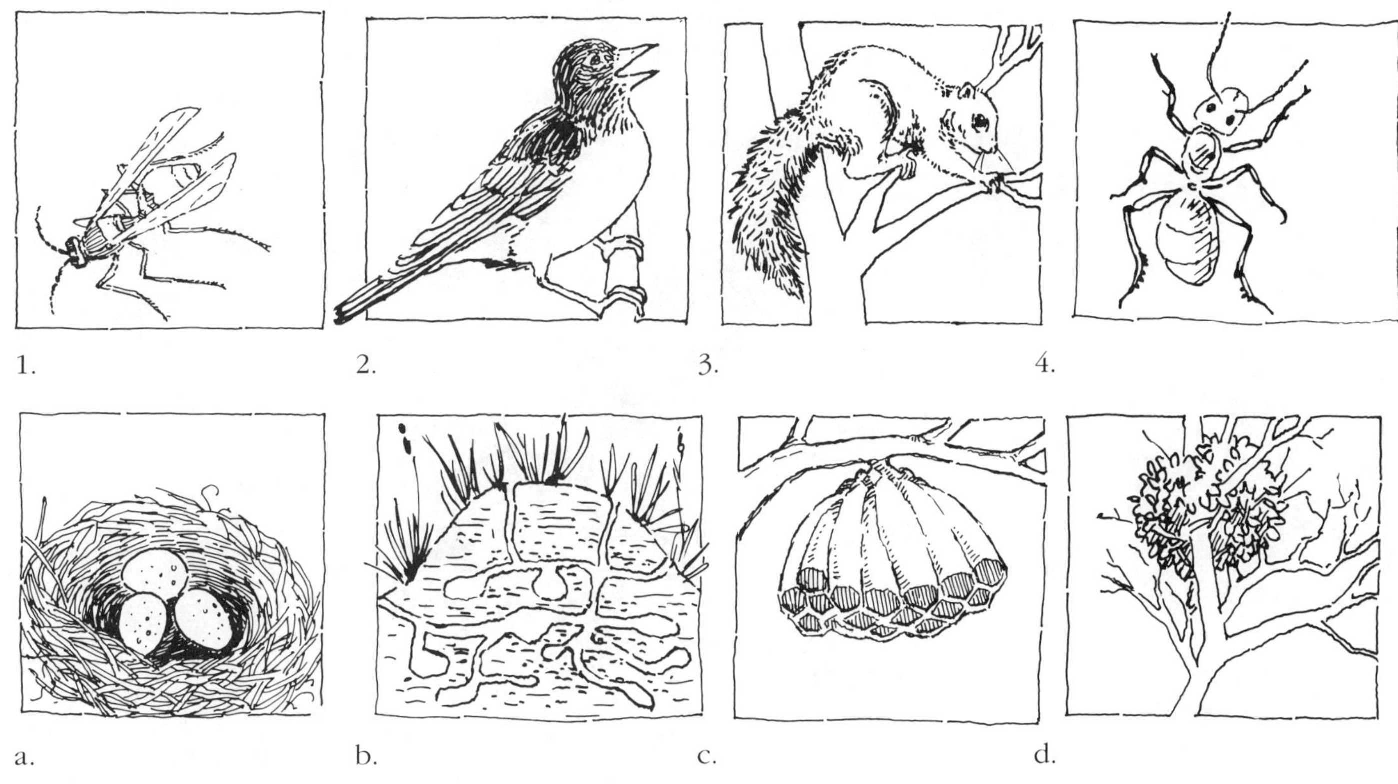


*ANSWERS: 1c, 2a, 3d, 4b*

## Mini Egg Collection

You've heard of Easter egg hunts? Here's an egg hunt with a difference. Get your magnifying glass and spotting eyes ready. See how many insect eggs you can find. Look under stones, in rotting wood, on leaves or twigs, and underground around your home—places where eggs are hidden from mammals, birds, and insects that might eat them.

Not sure what will hatch out of your eggs? Hatch them in a bugarium. (Page 73 tells you how.)

Butterfly egg

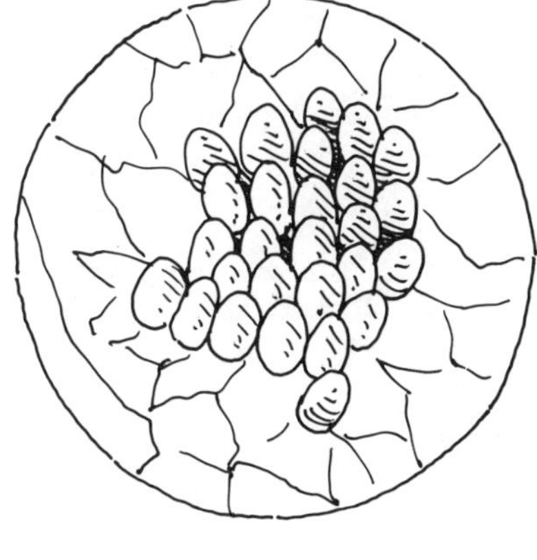

Ladybug eggs

Record your observations about birds in your journal.
Feathers are...
Bill is...
They eat...
Nesting place is...
Kind of nest is...

## Weed Birds?

Starlings, house sparrows, and pigeons are so common, and sometimes so pesky, that people call them nuisance birds. They all came from other places. They all like city life.

"Weed birds" are neat to study. Because they are fairly tame, you can get close enough to watch their behavior. Check them out! What can you discover?

Pigeon

Starling

House sparrow

## Wonderful Weeds

Wonderful weeds, not dainty wildflowers, survive in vacant lots, alleys, and roadsides in the city. They need no pampering. They grow in soil packed almost as hard as concrete. Look for weeds in the city. Look for the features that help them survive.

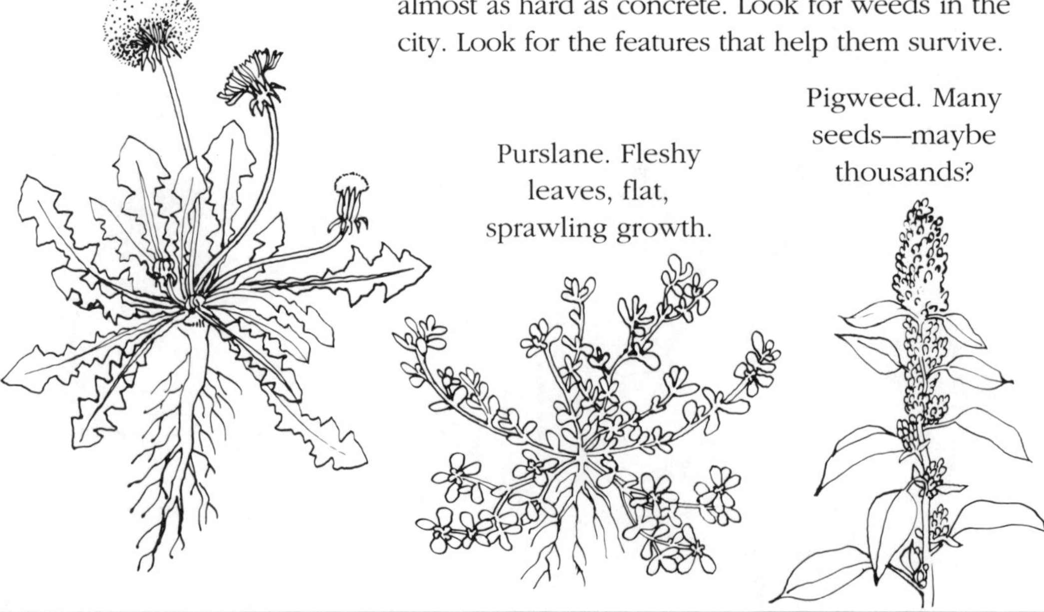

Dandelion. Tap root, parachute seeds.

Purslane. Fleshy leaves, flat, sprawling growth.

Pigweed. Many seeds—maybe thousands?

## Who Am I?

My long, scaly body
Has gold stripes on green.
Through the grasses
I slither
Passing unseen.

My fork-tipped red tongue
Flicks out here and there.
It is tasting my world
Of prey-scented air.

I silently wait for
My lunch to arrive.
I coil and lunge quickly.
Then eat it alive!

My jaws have a hinge
So my mouth opens wide.
Yum, yum, what a feast.
Watch the lump move
inside!

Who am I?

*ANSWER: Garter snake.*

Garter snakes can be found in damp, grassy places even in the city.

# Helping Habitat

Before people came to this area, plants and animals had all the space. As people moved in, wildlife got pushed out. It doesn't have to be that way. We can make it easier for wildlife to share space with us, even in the cities.

The way to help wildlife is to help habitat.

Who can help? Kids, families, neighborhoods, school classes, *anyone who cares*!

What can you do? Meet the four important needs of plants and animals in your habitat.

Where can you do this? Yards, whole neighborhoods, vacant lots, school grounds, or anywhere there's a free space.

## What Animals and Plants Need

Animals are no different from people. Animals need food to eat. They need water. They need somewhere to live. They need cover to hide in to be safe from harm. These things make up their habitat.

FOOD + WATER + HOME SITES + COVER = GOOD ANIMAL HABITAT

These animal needs, including some water, can be provided by plants. But what do plants need to grow? They need sunlight to make food. They need water. They need soil. They need space to grow. Plants and animals have similar needs.

LIGHT + WATER + SOIL + GROWING SPACE = GOOD PLANT HABITAT

A tiny island of green can attract insects, birds, and other animals. Sometimes these green islands are hard for the animals to find. Suppose all the neighbors along a whole street work at "habitat-helping"? There's a better chance the animals will find a place that suits them. Can you persuade your neighbors to be "neighborly to wildlife"?

Habitat-helping has a bonus. When you make habitat better for animals, it is more pleasant for people, too!

A wildlife smile to everyone who does any project that helps habitat—read on for ideas.

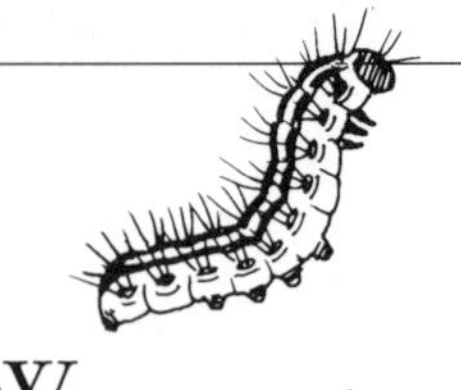

Want to read more about it?
*Gardening With Wildlife. The Official Backyard Habitat Planning and Planting Kit.*
The National Wildlife Federation.
A planning and planting kit.

## Helping Habitat—The First Step

Make a sketch map of the existing habitat you'd like to improve. Keep a log book. What insects, amphibians, reptiles, birds, or mammals live in the habitat right now? When are they active? What do they do? Which places do they seem to like? Once you know what's there, you can plan to improve the habitat so it fills the four wildlife needs. If a place is good right now, leave it alone!

The projects can be small or large. Here are some ideas:

- Set up butterfly window boxes or gardens.
- Plant food and cover for the birds.
- Make a birdbath.
- Build a birdhouse.
- Collect a brush pile to make an animal shelter.
- Compost leaves, grass clippings, and leftovers to make rich soil in which to grow your new plants. (See page 67 for more about compost.)

1.

## Water! Water!

Nothing can live without water. Here are some ideas to provide water in your habitat:

1. Punch a small hole in the bottom of a plastic bucket. Thread a piece of string through the hole and let water drip slowly. Hang the bucket on a tree branch above your birdbath. The sound of drips will attract birds.

2. Line a hole with plastic or a rubber sheet. Use a flowerpot as a toad shelter. Is there a basking and shelter rock for garter snakes?

3. Place an old towel in a shallow dish to wick up water for insects.

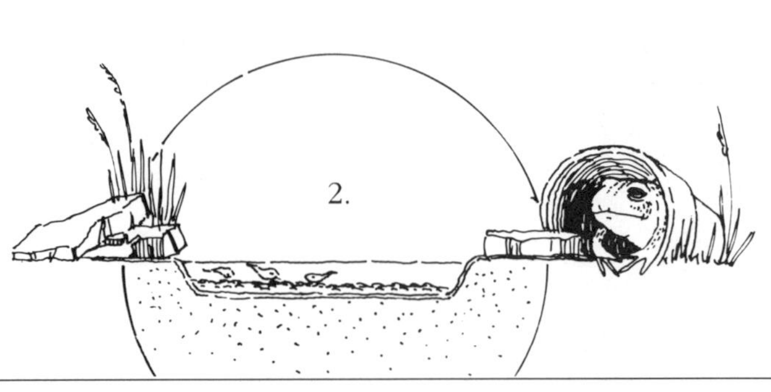

# Home Sweet Home

Very tidy places may please humans, but they don't suit wildlife. Mammals and birds need tangly places to hide. They need safe, hidden places to build a home-sweet-home. Here's how you can help.

1. Shelter for birds and small mammals.

2. Good home sites.

3. Cover and safe travel routes. (Is it your job to mow or water? This makes the job smaller and easier!)

4. Perches.

5. Birdhouse. Next best thing to dead trees with cavities!

6. Water is essential. Is it safe to get to?

7. Safe hiding should be near, but not too close. Beware of lurking cats!

8. Different levels suit different creatures.

9. Edges are the best of both worlds! There's always more wildlife where two kinds of living space meet.

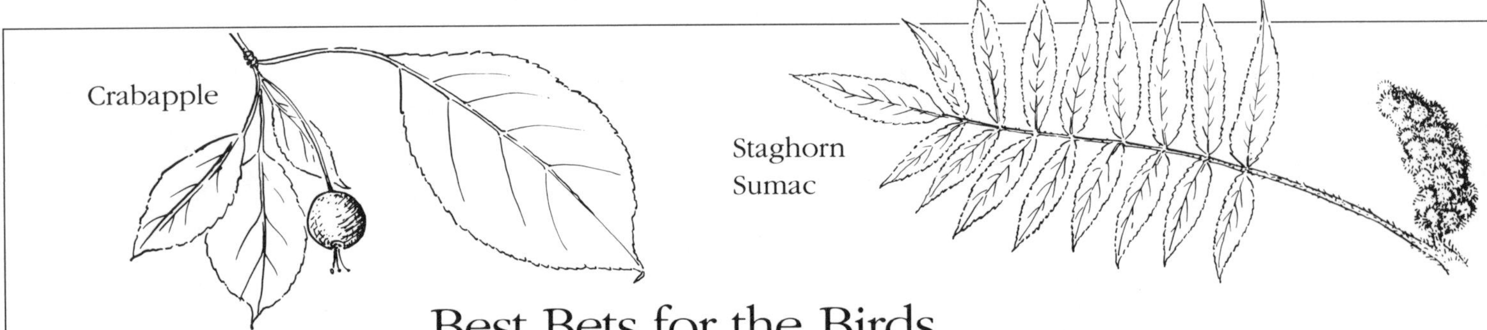


# Best Bets for the Birds

Birds flock to trees and shrubs with tasty berries. They relish sunflower seeds and thistle seeds if you can leave patches of these plants in your yard.

Chokecherry

## Fast, Fly-In Feasts

Sometimes a habitat does not provide enough food for birds, especially in winter. Help the birds by feeding them until the berry bushes grow! Here are some ideas for feeders. More birds will turn up to check out your feeder if you fill it regularly. Be faithful—the birds rely on you!

Fill pine cones with peanut butter and roll in bird seed to attract nuthatches. Hang suet hung in a net bag to entice woodpeckers. Stuff suet-seed mix into holes drilled in a log for chickadees.

## Gourmet Goodies

Birds don't all have the same favorite foods. Try different foods in your feeder and see who comes to dine. Here are some good foods to try:

- black sunflower seed
- thistle
- millet
- fruit (bits of apple peel, raisins, half an orange)
- suet (free from most supermarket meat departments)

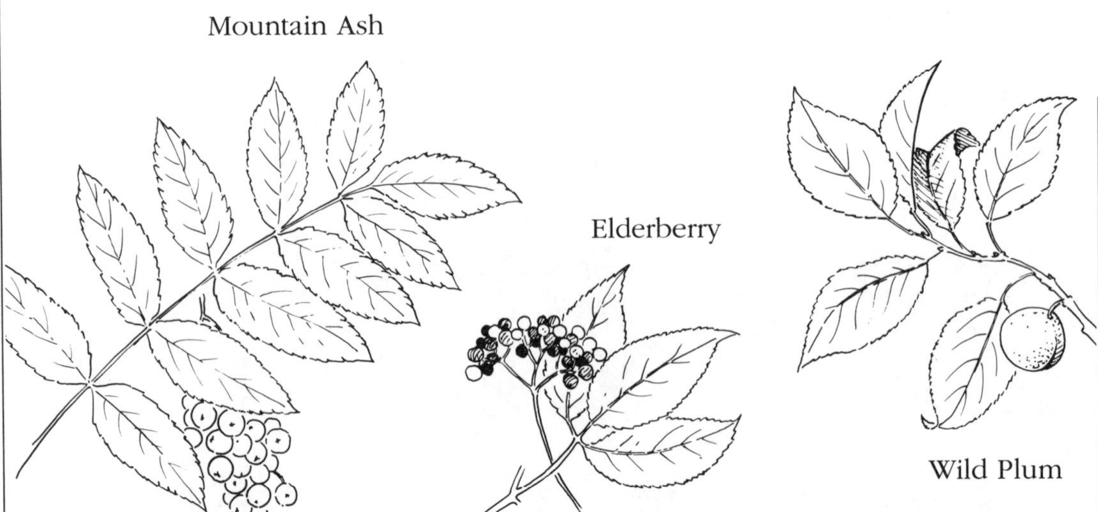

**A** wildlife smile! Some birds are insect monitors. They control aphids, mosquitoes, and other over-plentiful insects without pesticides. That's a good deal!

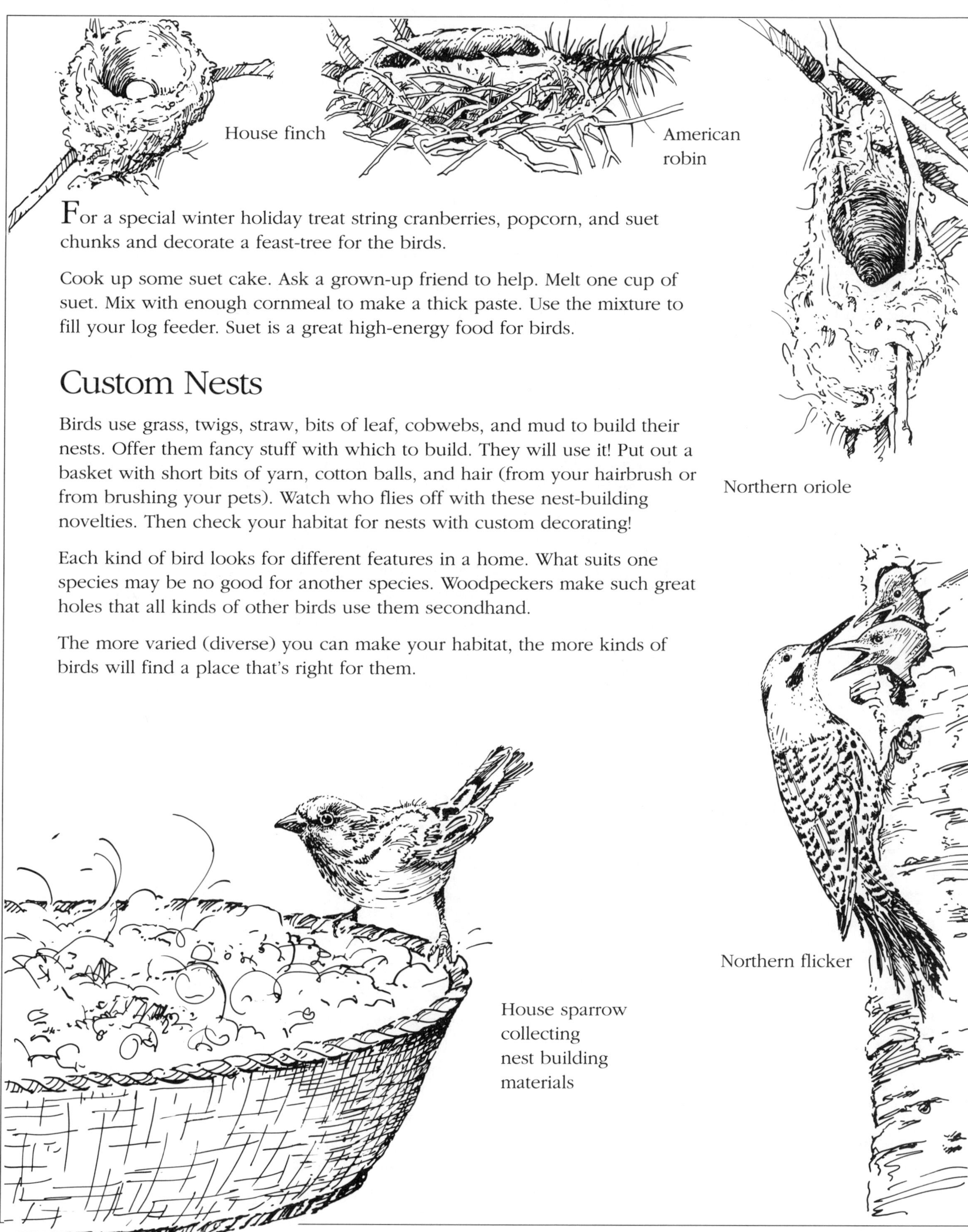


For a special winter holiday treat string cranberries, popcorn, and suet chunks and decorate a feast-tree for the birds.

Cook up some suet cake. Ask a grown-up friend to help. Melt one cup of suet. Mix with enough cornmeal to make a thick paste. Use the mixture to fill your log feeder. Suet is a great high-energy food for birds.

## Custom Nests

Birds use grass, twigs, straw, bits of leaf, cobwebs, and mud to build their nests. Offer them fancy stuff with which to build. They will use it! Put out a basket with short bits of yarn, cotton balls, and hair (from your hairbrush or from brushing your pets). Watch who flies off with these nest-building novelties. Then check your habitat for nests with custom decorating!

Each kind of bird looks for different features in a home. What suits one species may be no good for another species. Woodpeckers make such great holes that all kinds of other birds use them secondhand.

The more varied (diverse) you can make your habitat, the more kinds of birds will find a place that's right for them.

A wildlife smile to a Fort Collins teacher and a lot of kids who build nest boxes for the Cherokee Park Bluebird Trail. The bluebird nest box described here is this teacher's design. It would be a good box to build if you live in an open mountain area.

## Hole-Nester's Haven

Here is a project to do with a grown-up friend. This house is for bluebirds.

**You'll need:**

- 5 foot length of 1" x 6" pine (woodwork isn't metric yet!)
- 2 1-1/2" duplex nails
- 12 2" ring shank nails
- saw, hammer, and a hole saw

If the wood cracks as you nail, don't worry about it. Cracks won't make any difference to the birds! If you want a neater box, you can pre-drill before you nail.

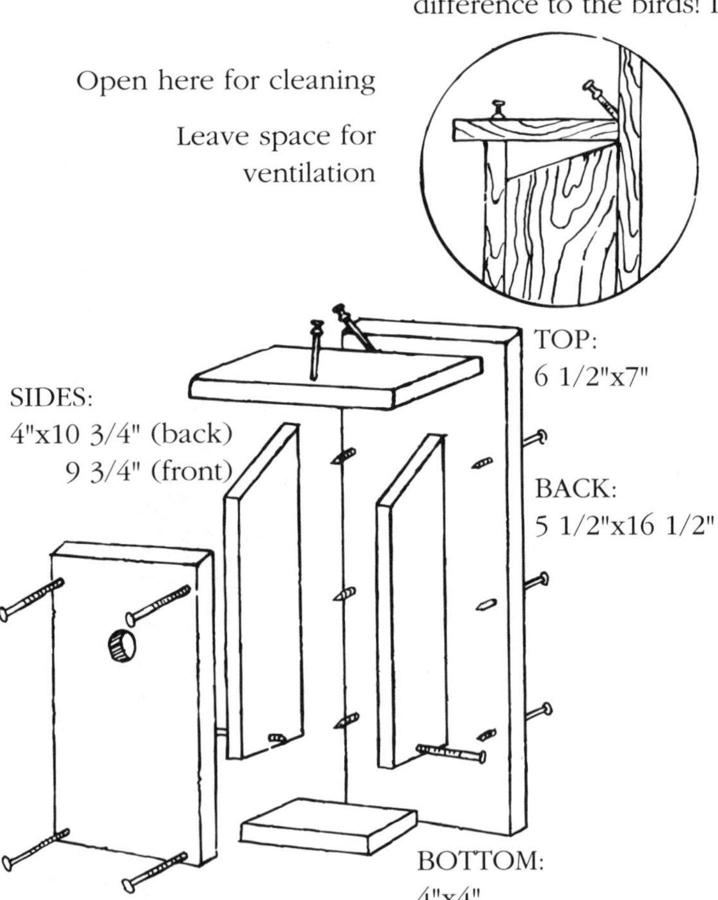


Entrance. (1-1/2" diameter and 6" above the floor)

Other birds will use nest boxes if the entrance hole is the right size and the right height above the floor. All the boxes can be made according to the same general pattern, but with custom sizes. Try these for houses for other birds.

**chickadee:**
floor 4" x 4"; hole 1-1/8"; hole height 6"–8"

**house finch:**
floor 5" x 5"; hole 1-1/2"; hole height 6"

**flicker:**
floor 7" x 7"; hole 2-1/2"; hole height 14"–16"

Choose the location for your box with care. It should be at the best height for the bird you want to attract. (Chickadee, 6–15 feet above the ground; house finch, 5–10 feet; and flicker, 6–20 feet.) Place the house out of the full sun. Point the door away from wind and rain.

Don't be disappointed if your house is not occupied right away. Give the birds time! You may need to experiment with the location, too. Don't be surprised if squirrels move into your flicker house, or house sparrows like the house finch box. After all, how are they to know which boxes are for them?

**Larva:**
(more than one is larvae)
an early stage in the life of an insect

# Butterfly Gardens

Plan a garden that grows butterflies. It can be done! Flowers with plentiful nectar will entice adult butterflies to feed. To really *grow* butterflies in your garden, plant flowers and shrubs that butterfly **larvae** feed on. Spare some leaves for hungry, munching caterpillars to eat. The reward? The larvae will grow up, and you will have a garden full of swallowtails, fritillaries, skippers, and many other butterflies.

Painted lady butterfly

Check out which flowers, shrubs, and trees attract butterflies in your neighborhood. Are the flowers good butterfly perches? Do they have a lot of nectar? Or do they have lots of tiny flowers close together that make nectar sipping easier?

See plants that attract butterflies at Denver Botanic Gardens (11).

Remember, plants are more than food.

- They are basking places, where butterflies can soak up sun's rays to warm their flying muscles.
- They are shelter from wind and rain.
- They are places to overwinter.
- They are places for larvae to pupate (change inside) before hatching into adults.

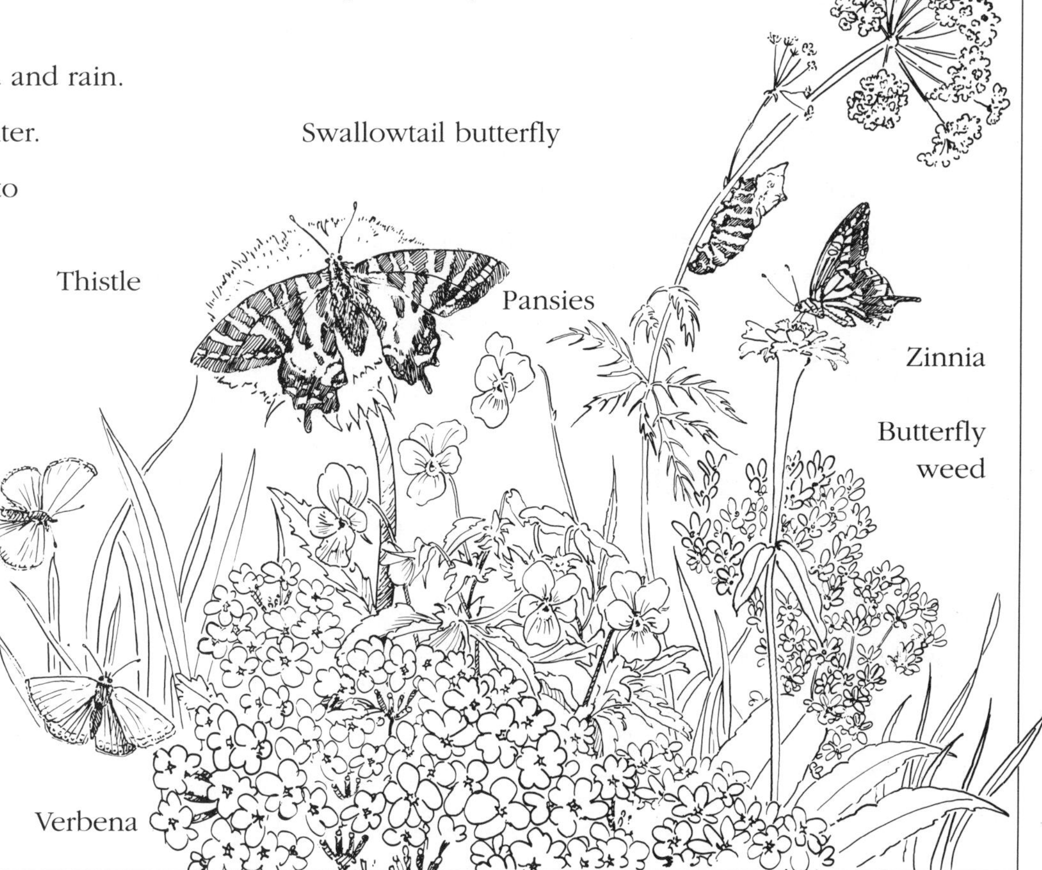

A wildlife smile! Butterflies are a sign of how healthy a habitat is. Lots of butterflies are proof that your area is not badly polluted.

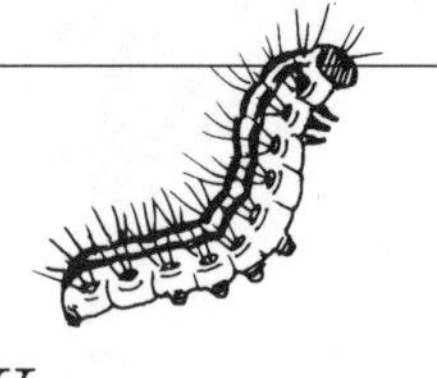

Want to know more about it?
*The Butterfly Garden.* Mathew Tekulsky. For good readers and grown-ups.
*Butterflies of the American West: A Coloring Album.* Paul A. Opler. To learn species.

Butterflies need water, too. They sip it with their long, straw-like mouths. Butterfly drinking fountains needn't be fancy—just any shallow water. Try these ideas for butterfly drinking fountains.

- Keep wet a patch of dirt or sand.
- Put a piece of burlap under a drippy tap to catch the water.
- Set an old sponge in a dish on a fence, wall, or windowsill. Wet the sponge every day.

## Bats About Bats

Bats are good neighbors. Let them share your habitat. They fly at dusk and feast on mosquitoes and other insects. Encourage them to stay by building a bat box in which they can roost.

You'll need same materials as for the bird box (page 32) The bat box is almost like the bird box. Here are the differences:

- The sides are cut square (no ventilation spaces) to make a dark box.
- There is no hole in the front.
- The entrance is a slit in the base.

Before you nail the box together make shallow saw-cuts to roughen the inside surface. The rough surface will help bats grip with their claws.

Cedar fence pickets also make good bird and bat boxes. They weather to a soft gray color. Use the rough surface inside a bat box, so the bats can hang on. Cedar is a harder wood than pine. You may need to pre-drill before you nail.

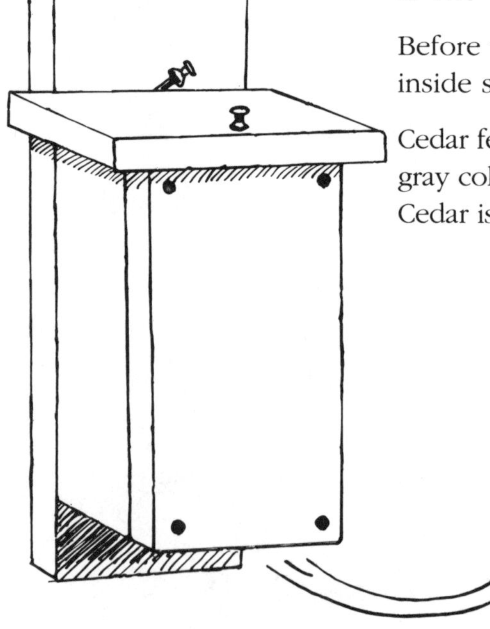

# GREAT GRASSLANDS

Before cities were built along the Front Range, grasslands stretched east across Colorado. Trees were rare. Because the climate was (and still is) dry, trees grew in flood plains and along creeks and rivers.

Animals of the High Plains adapted to a treeless, grasslands life. Many animals lived underground. Birds nested on the ground. Dwellers on the plains found new ways to escape enemies.

When people settled in Colorado, they changed the land. They plowed the shortgrass prairie to plant wheat and oats. They grew different kinds of grasses to cut for hay. They planted turf-grasses in parks and lawns. These fields, meadows, and parks are grassy places, but are different from the grasslands they replaced.

Preview life on the grasslands and in other Colorado habitats at the Denver Museum of Natural History (12).

## Holes, Holes, Holes

Underground is an important place in the treeless grasslands. Deep in the soil it is cool and moist in summer. It is warmer than the surface in winter. The ground shelters animals from drying winds or crashing hail and rain. It protects them against fast-moving grass fires. It gives them a home.

Check out underground animal activity by being a hole-hunter. The best way to meet the hole-owner is to sit quietly and watch! Look for these animals that live in holes:

❑ A fox makes several holes close together.

❑ A badger hole has an oval shape like the badger's body.

❑ A bullsnake takes over holes that pocket gophers dig.

❑ Grass spiders weave funnel-shaped webs. Tap her web gently to see the spider rush out! Does she think you are a meal?

Foxhole

**Community:** all the plants and animals that live together in a habitat

## Scrambling for Safety

**Unscramble the letters to find grasslands animals. Match them with the escape or self-protection they use.**

1. KSNUK
2. OBX URTELT
3. ENORHD DZILRA
4. DWOMAERALK
5. SKEANTTLERA
6. PIEARRI DGO

a. Squirts blood from the eyes.
b. Hides in hole.
c. Hides in its shell.
d. Squirts smelly liquid from tail gland.
e. Sits tight and is camouflaged.
f. Rattles its tail.

*ANSWERS: 1. Skunk d. 2. Box turtle c. 3. Horned lizard a. 4. Meadowlark e. 5. Rattlesnake f. 6. Prairie dog b.*

## Big Town on the Prairie

Towns have been on the grasslands since long before people came—prairie dog towns! But prairie dogs are not the only animals that live in the towns. They are just one of the species that lives in this **community.**

Prairie dogs move and loosen soil as they dig their burrows. The work of prairie dogs makes it easier for neighbors to move in. Burrowing owls (1) borrow a chamber to build a nest. Rattlesnakes (2) take shelter and hunt a meal. Coyotes (3) and foxes seek unwary prey on the ground. Hawks (4) and eagles hunt from the sky, watching for a meal. Turkey vultures (5) circle overhead. They will scavenge meat that others leave.

When one kind of animal, such as the black-footed ferret, disappears from a community, it changes the balance of life there.

## Pronghorns and Jackrabbits

Why is a pronghorn like a jackrabbit? (This isn't a joke!) There are several answers:

■ Both are herbivores. Both mammals eat grass and small bushes. They must find food without being found by a predator that wants to eat them.

■ Both have eyes set high on the sides of their heads. That way, they can eat and watch for enemies at the same time.

■ Both use speed to escape their enemies. The grasslands have few hiding places for large mammals. Young pronghorn and jackrabbits are born ready to run. Though still wobbly, they can escape from danger if they need to.

■ Both have white tails that flash warnings.

Two other animals used to be found in prairie dog towns. Bison liked to roll, or wallow, in the dusty diggings. Wild bison no longer live in Colorado. Black-footed ferrets, predators who ate prairie dogs, are an endangered species. Only about 150 of them are left alive in the whole world.

A prairie dog at his listening post (A) is alert for enemies. Prairie dog homes have a chamber that stays dry during floods (B), a toilet chamber (C), and a sleeping chamber with a nest (D). A mother stays with her babies in a nursery chamber (E). One of the many entrances (F) is a quick escape route.

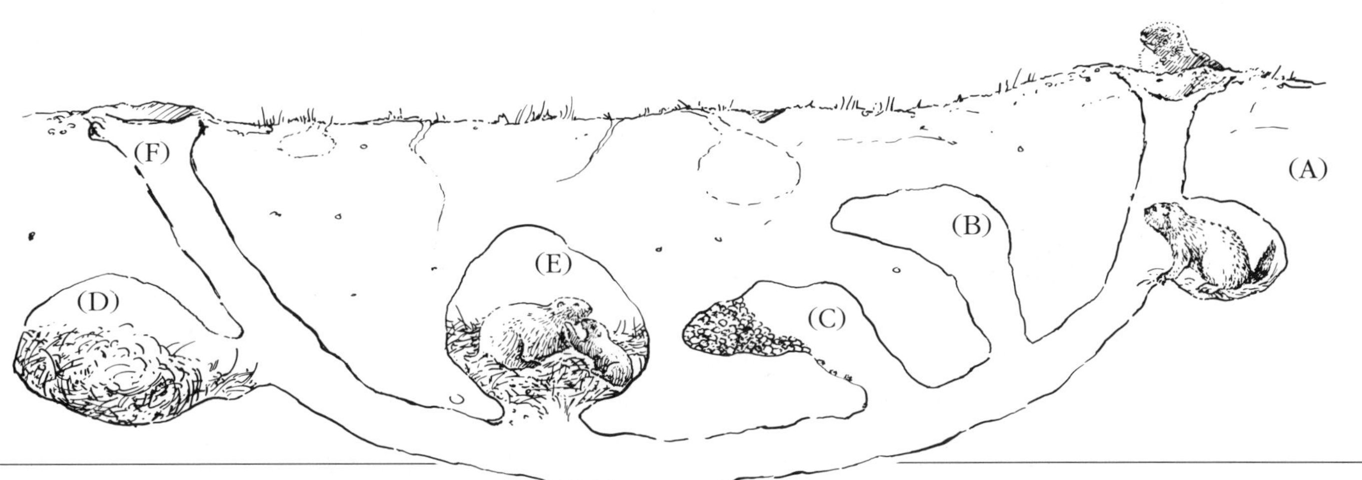

## The Munch Bunch

Can you believe that millions of munching teeth keep the shortgrass prairie looking the way it does?

Grass and grazers go together. Grass keeps growing when its tips are snipped off. It grows between each node and gets even thicker with snipping. Grazers do the mowing on the grasslands. They have teeth designed for the job.

If grasslands are grazed by too many animals, the grass is cut or nibbled so short it has no energy left to grow. That's why bison used to migrate across the High Plains. They moved to new food supplies while the old grasslands grew lush again.

## Birds of Open Places

Birds of the grasslands have few trees or bushes to nest in. Perches are hard to find. The birds must adapt to a ground-and-sky life.

❑ The lark bunting sings while in flight to attract a mate.

❑ The prairie chicken gathers on booming grounds to find a mate. Why *booming grounds*? For the strange sounds the male makes with its inflated air sac.

❑ The western meadowlark hides its nest in tufts of grass. Its brown, streaky back conceals the sitting bird.

❑ The prairie falcon nests on the steep cliffs of the High Plains.

Lark Bunting is Colorado's State Bird

Comanche National Grasslands, south and southeast of La Junta (24).

Check out the grasshoppers in your grassy neighborhood and add your findings to your journal.

## Great Grazing Grasshoppers!

One grasshopper doesn't eat much grass. But a crowd of them together can eat as much as a bison. When too many grasshoppers live in a small area the food runs out. The grasshoppers fly in large swarms to find food somewhere else on the plains.

## Ant Guide Book

Imagine an exploring ant trekking across a park! For her size, that's quite a journey. A tall grass stem might seem like a mighty redwood to an ant! A boulder might seem like Long's Peak!

Mark out a patch of grass a meter square. What hazards would ants meet on their journey across your square? Why not make them a guide book? Use numbered popsicle sticks to mark special features on this treacherous trail.

1. Beware of sticky plant!
2. Good food here!
3. Watch out—deep lake!
4. Ant lion trap!
5. Watch out for toad!

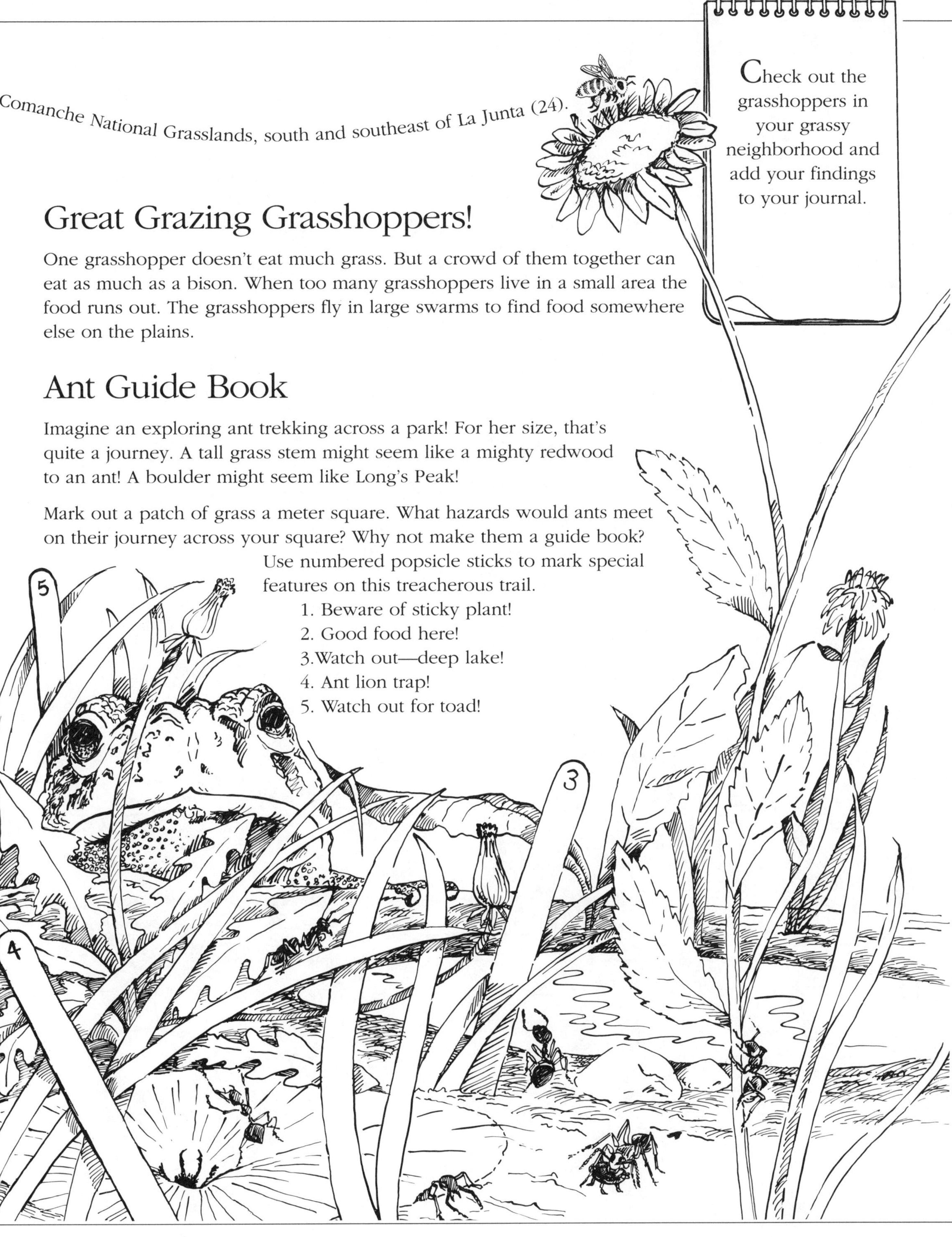

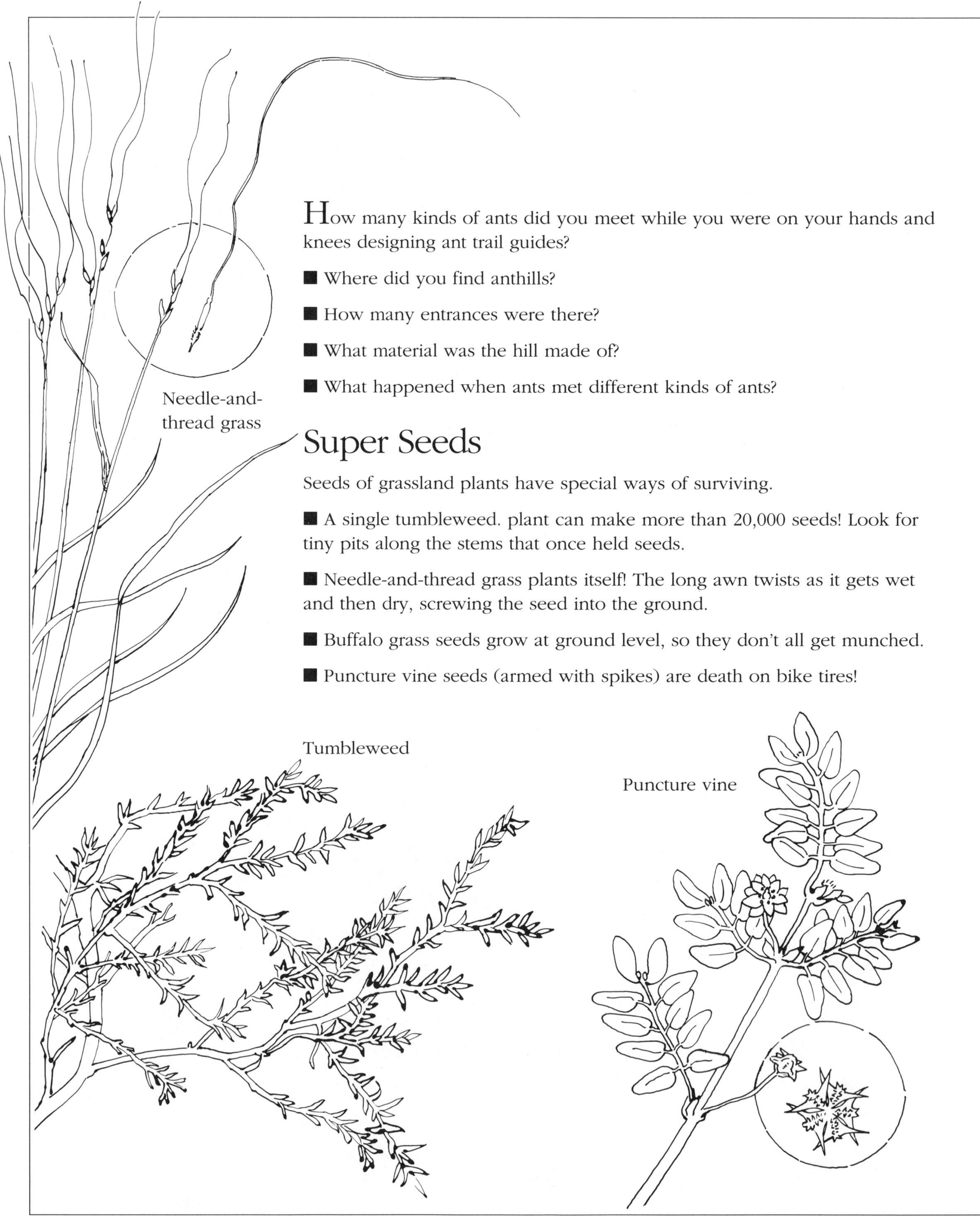


How many kinds of ants did you meet while you were on your hands and knees designing ant trail guides?

- Where did you find anthills?
- How many entrances were there?
- What material was the hill made of?
- What happened when ants met different kinds of ants?

## Super Seeds

Seeds of grassland plants have special ways of surviving.

- A single tumbleweed. plant can make more than 20,000 seeds! Look for tiny pits along the stems that once held seeds.
- Needle-and-thread grass plants itself! The long awn twists as it gets wet and then dry, screwing the seed into the ground.
- Buffalo grass seeds grow at ground level, so they don't all get munched.
- Puncture vine seeds (armed with spikes) are death on bike tires!

# WONDERFUL WETLANDS

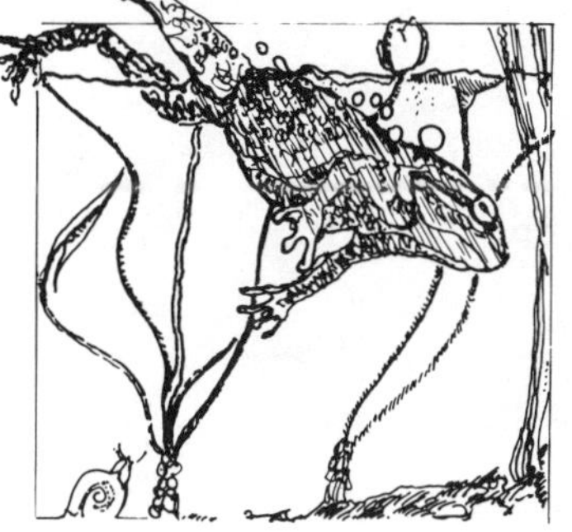

Everything alive needs water. Nothing can live without it. No wonder wet places are great for wildlife! All watery habitats do not suit all animals and plants equally well. Each kind of water animal and water plant fits its own chosen habitat. Some plants and animals are specialists. Perhaps they can live only in the splash zone of a waterfall, or the surface layer of a pond. Other animals and plants (generalists) are more tolerant. They can survive in a wider range of conditions. This crossword puzzle is full of watery places to explore.

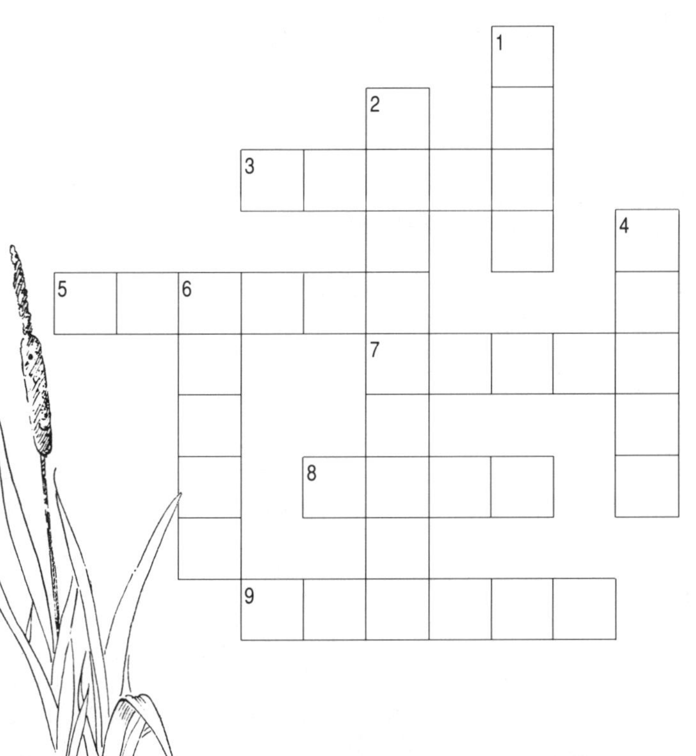


ACROSS

3. Coal _ _ _ _ _, Cherry _ _ _ _ _, and Clear _ _ _ _ _ are Front Range rivers.
5. A short-lasting wet place that forms after rain or snow then dries up in the sun.
7. The South Platte is an important Colorado _ _ _ _ _ for wildlife.
8. Shallow water, home to frogs and turtles, where rooted plants grow all the way across.
9. Water that bubbles up from the ground.

DOWN

1. Fresh water that is too deep for plants to grow all the way across.
2. A man-made lake with a dam. Its banks show signs of big changes in water level.
4. Soggy ground where cattails grow.
6. Slow-flowing water in a man-made channel, used for irrigation and drainage.

WORD LIST: Pond, Ditch, River, Puddle, Creek, Marsh, Lake, Spring, Reservoir

Are you ready to check out some watery habitats? Take a grown-up friend along for safety.

- Is the water still or flowing?
- Is the water cold or warm?
- Are the banks steep or gently sloping?
- Are there holes in the banks that could be homes?
- What grows along the banks?

All these things influence which wildlife you will find. Animals are picky about their needs. Swamp or puddle life would not suit trout! Catfish and their babies would wash away in the swift currents of a fast-flowing river.

*ANSWERS:*
*1. Lake, 2. Reservoir, 3. Creek, 4. Marsh, 5. Puddle, 6. Ditch, 7. River, 8. Pond, 9. Spring*

# Ponds and Lakes

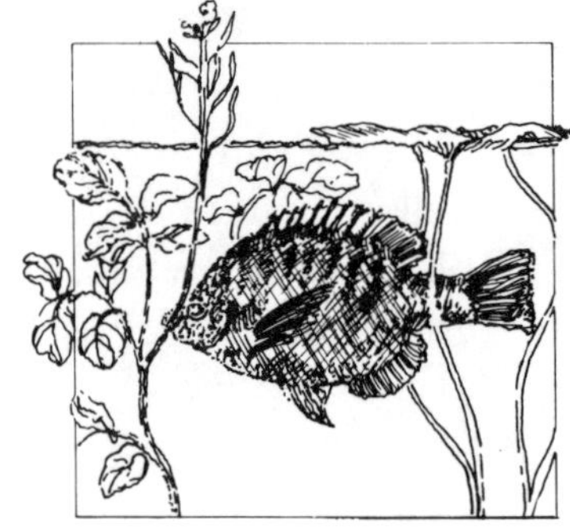

## A Look at Still Water Habitats

Animals that live in lakes, ponds, and marshes often choose particular parts of them to live in.
When you wildwatch, check out these habitats:

- surface film,
- open water,
- muddy or gravelly bottoms,
- undersides of rocks (Put rocks back gently!),
- shoreline.

## Breath of Life

All animals need oxygen to stay alive. People and animals that live on land get oxygen from the air around them. Animals that live in water must adapt their ways of breathing. There are many ways to do it. Check them out as you explore.

- ❑ A water beetle traps an air bubble on its hairy underside and dives with it.
- ❑ A pond snail comes to the surface and breathes air through a breathing hole.
- ❑ A water scorpion breathes air through a long tube, like a snorkel.

Watch lake life from boardwalk trails over the water at Barr Lake State Park (10).

**Amphibian:** an animal that has two lives—one in water, one on land.

## Cattail Supermarket

Native Americans used cattails for food. A cattail marsh was nature's pantry.

- Young shoots tasted like asparagus. They were eaten raw or cooked.
- Young flowers were eaten like corn on the cob.
- Starchy winter roots were peeled and cooked like potatoes.

Native Americans gathered the fluffy seed "down" to make pillows and to pad the cradleboards where their babies slept. They also used this down for baby diapers.

Check out the cattails in your marsh. Who is using them now?

- Who hatched here?
- Who lives here?
- Are eyes watching you? Who is checking you out?

## Opera of Spring

*Ten bullfrogs croak the bass*
*In their harsh ribits deep.*
*Twenty leopard frogs are tenors*
*Peep, peep, peeping as they leap.*

*Five mallards quack the alto*
*As they swim across the pond,*
*While a robin sings his descant*
*From a lacy willow frond.*

*What's this rhythmic, lilting lullaby*
*The marsh dwellers sing*
*In the mossy, musky evening?*
*It's the opera of spring.*

Meet an **amphibian**!

**Food chain:** the energy pathway from sun to plants to animals. Energy from the sun powers everything.

## Birds of the Wetlands

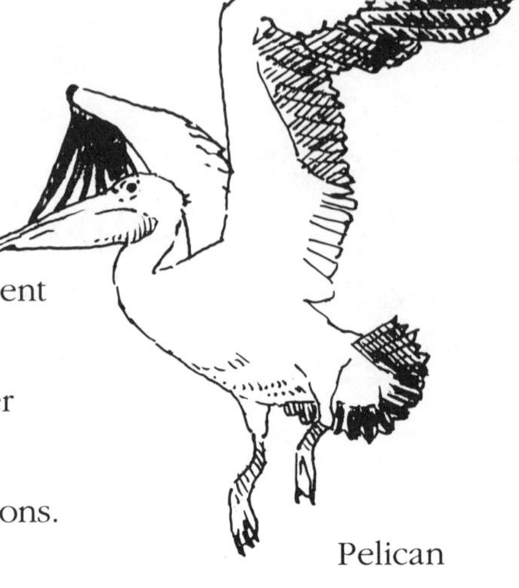

Pelican

Bills, legs, and feet tell the story of how different birds are adapted to get their food.

- Long legged herons wade deep in the water and stab fish with their pointed bills.
- Ospreys grip fish with their strong curved talons.
- Pelicans scoop fish in their pouches.

Look for other types of bills, legs, and feet as you wildwatch. How do they help the bird get food?

Muskrat

## Mighty Mouth

Which humming insect bites people who visit ponds? CLUES: Mouth like hypodermic needle! Only the female bites. She needs protein from blood to be able to lay her eggs. The male sucks plant juices, not blood.

What good are mosquitoes? Look around to see who eats them! They are an important link in the **food chains** of the pond.

SUN=GREEN ALGAE=MOSQUITO LARVA=FISH=OSPREY IS A FOOD CHAIN

## Telltale Tails

A pet dog would have you believe that tails are just for wagging. But pond animals have tails that do all kinds of things. See if you can find these, and other talented tails, when you explore.

- ❑ Muskrat. Uses its tail as a steering rudder.
- ❑ Dragonfly nymph. Jet of water propels the insect forward.
- ❑ Dragonfly. Its tail is the egg-laying tube.

Dragonfly nymph

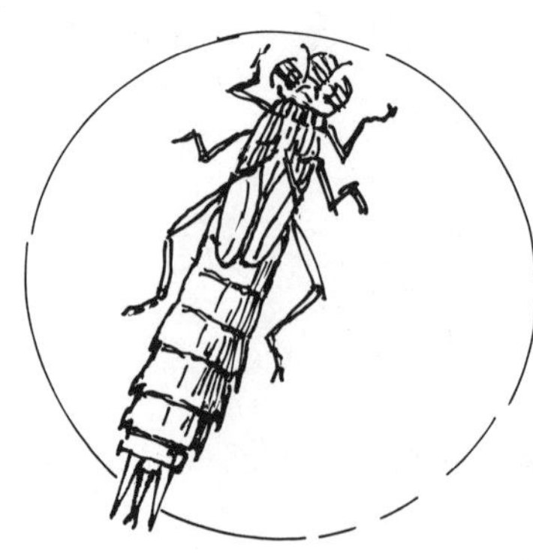

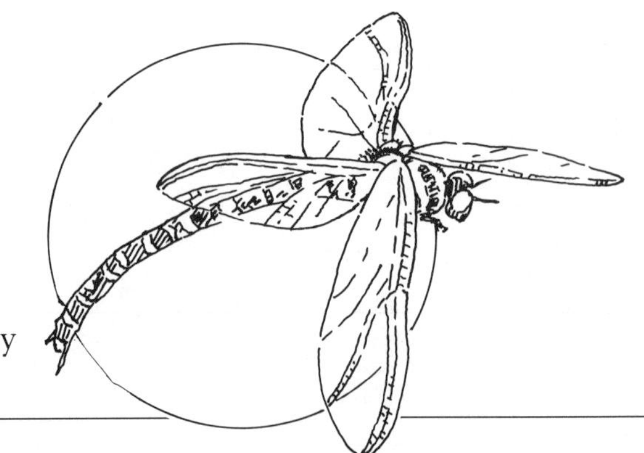

Dragonfly

# Turtle Talk

You can't ask a turtle about its turtle-life.
Find out by reading about or watching painted turtles.

**True (T) or False (F)?**

____ Painted turtles rest on sunny logs.

____ They find food on land.

____ Turtles can crawl out of their shells.

____ Turtles lay their eggs in holes along pond banks.

*ANSWERS:*
*1. True. Turtles bask in the sun to warm their bodies so they can move faster and digest their food better.*
*2. False. Painted turtles eat plants and animals in the water.*
*3. False. Turtles can't crawl out of their shells. These mobile homes are part of the turtle's body. The ribs are fused (joined) to the bony plates of the shell. The plates grow bigger as the turtle grows bigger.*
*4. True. Mother turtles come on land and dig holes in which to lay their eggs.*

# Perfect Pet

Imagine a pet this long ___ , with one foot and lots of arms, who can live in a peanut butter jar! There is such an animal! Meet *Hydra*.

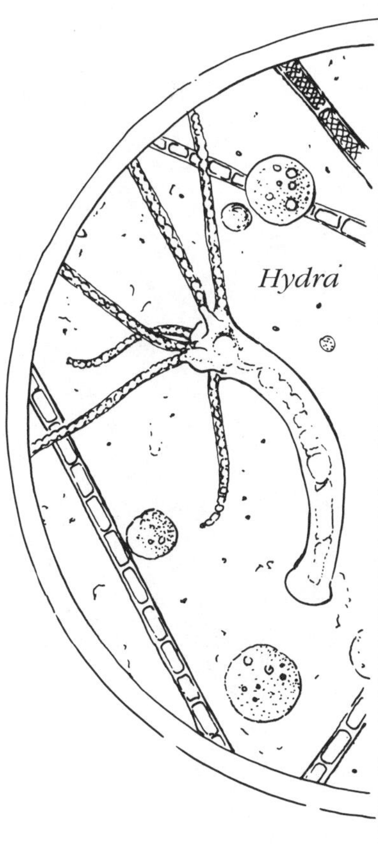


You can often find *Hydra* in shallow, sunny areas of clean ponds, streams, or lakes. Collect water, water plants, and bottom debris from several shallow places (use several jars). Keep on a windowsill that is bright but not sunny. After a few days check your jars with a magnifying glass. Look on the brightest side of your mini-ponds. Chances are you have pet *Hydra* to study.

Remove one-third of the water every few days. Replace it with fresh *pond water*. (Don't use tap water. It has chlorine in it.) The fresh pond water will have lots of new food for your hydras. Put the *Hydras* back in their real ponds when you are through studying them.

Watch how the *Hydras* move. What do they eat? Keep notes about them in your journal.

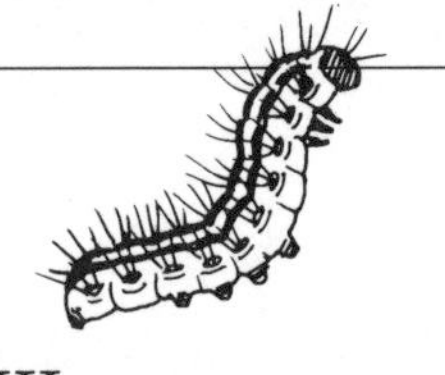

Want to read more about it?
*Pets in a Jar. Collecting and Caring for Small Wild Animals.*
Seymour Simon.
For more details on windowsill ponds.
*A Golden Guide to Pond Life.*
George K. Reid.
To identify your pond finds.

# Pond in a Jar

**Try keeping a pond in a jar.**
**You'll need:**

- large jar or fish tank
- washed aquarium gravel
- a couple of rocks
- some pond weed
- pond water or tap water
- net or kitchen strainer
- light-colored pan or bucket

Put rocks, gravel, and pondweed in jar.

Fill jar or tank with water. Let it sit for a day to get rid of the chlorine. Add the animals. Keep on a bright, but not sunny windowsill.

Now for the animals! Go on a pond safari. Sweep through the pond water, especially near pond plants, with a net or kitchen strainer. Keep your finds in a light-colored pan or bucket. That way, it is easier to see what's what. Stick with small animals. Bigger insects, like dragonfly larvae, will eat everything else in your pond.

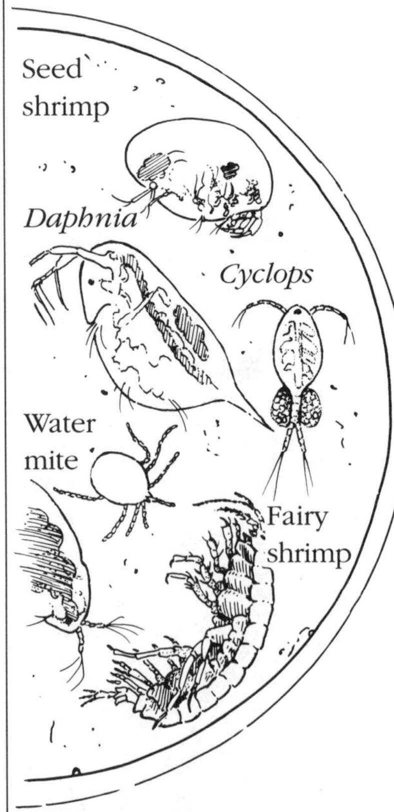

# Little Monsters

Would you like a monster zoo? Then collect a spoonful of pond water with a white plastic spoon. Those specks darting about are little monsters! Look at them with a magnifying glass.

You may find a mighty hunter in your spoonful of water: a mite with a bright orange body and eight legs. It sucks the body juices from water bugs when it is a larva. When it grows up, it eats whole water animals like the ones in your spoon. Yet it is only the size of this line - .

A pond in a jar gives you time to watch how the animals act. Write notes and draw pictures in your journal.

# Running Rivers

## A Look at Flowing Water Habitats

Many animals live in running water such as rivers or streams. In exchange for adapting to holding tight in the current, dinner comes to them! Dinner washes in from the banks of the stream when it rains. It travels downstream on the current. What is dinner? Dead animals, dead plants, and insects washed out of the soil or falling from the trees along the riverbanks are food.

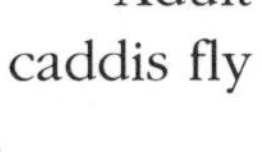


## Slippery Slime

Wading in a stream can be a slippery trip. The reason is algae, the green slime on the rocks. Algae is food for the plant eaters of streams and rivers. It also makes oxygen for water animals. So don't say YUCK! say GOOD GREEN SLIME!

## Peak to Prairie Highway

Streams, creeks, and rivers are like ribbons tying the mountaintops of Colorado to the prairies of Nebraska, Kansas, and Missouri. They are lines of life. Animals use them as cross-country highways to get from one living area to another.

People also enjoy the shade and beauty of rivers. But our presence can interfere with the lives of animals. That is why it is important to set aside some rivers to be forever wild.

We dam rivers because we need water. Animal and plant life is quite different below a dam, or in a reservoir, than the plant and animal life that used to live in the naturally flowing river. Can you think why?

Take a river walk at The Greenway and Nature Center of Pueblo on the Arkansas River (23).

Want to read more about it? *Signs Along the River. Learning to Read the National Landscape.* Kay Robertson. For more information on rivers.

## Choices

Different plants and animals live in different parts of creeks and rivers. Look for them in or near:

- rapids and waterfalls (Careful! Go with a grown-up.),
- quiet backwaters,
- under rocks (Put them back just as you found them!),
- in weeds,
- shallow, gravelly areas.

A river bank gives you clues about what lives on the river!

- Is your stream or river full of life?
- Is the water fresh? Clear? Cloudy? Full of silt?
- What grows on the banks?

Where there is vegetation, food drops in from the banks. Where there are clear-cut areas, silt washes in and clogs the river. Where the river collects water that has drained from streets, city gardens, or factories, there can be pollution.

## Underwater Flight?

Dippers belong in the air with their swift, direct flight. They belong on the riverbanks pecking for insects in the moss. They belong underwater, too. They "fly" through the water to reach the bottom, where they walk across rocks searching for food. Dippers are a good sign that a river is still clean and fresh, for these birds need pure, flowing water with plenty of caddis fly larvae, stone fly nymphs, and other insects to eat.

Use the river bike trails along the Cache La Poudre River, Fort Collins (4), Boulder Creek in

Dipper

A wildlife smile for the Platte River Greenway System. Restoring a city river makes great space for animals and humans alike!

## Master Builders

Caddis fly larvae build mobile homes. They use bits of material they find in the rivers and clear ponds they live in. They stick the bits together with "caddis fly glue." Check the caddis fly larvae in your river or pond:

- What are their cases made of?
- What shape are they?
- Are the cases heavy or light? (Some river caddis flies build heavier cases so they won't wash away in the current.)

## Fish Tales

A rainbow trout's body is sleek and streamlined. Water flows past and hardly makes any ripples. That is why trout can swim swiftly upstream against the current.

A pumpkinseed sunfish looks skinny from the front and round from the side—not streamlined. Narrow fish like this can swim gracefully among water weeds. They would be swept away if they swam broadside to a strong current. Sunfish live in slow rivers, lakes, and ponds.

Check out the fish you find. How do their body shapes fit the places they live?

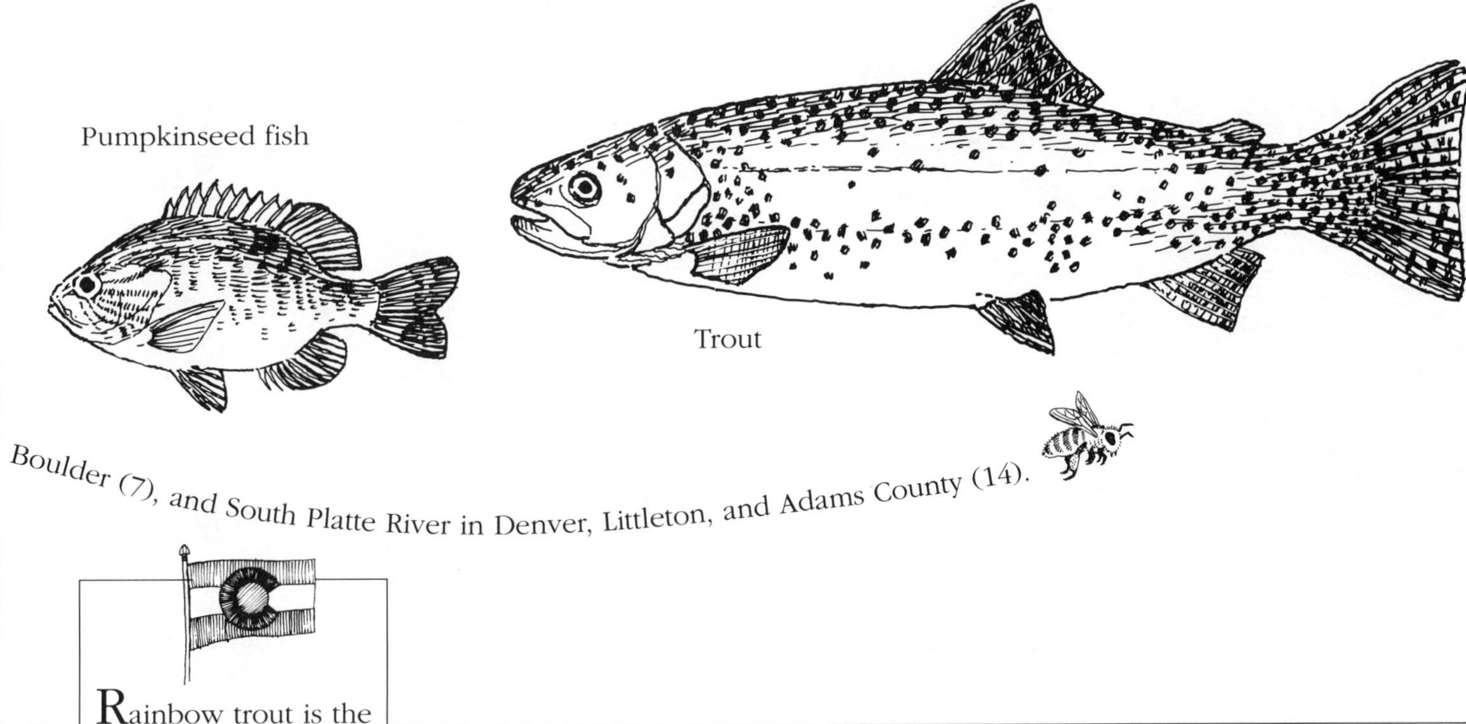

Pumpkinseed fish

Trout

Boulder (7), and South Platte River in Denver, Littleton, and Adams County (14).

Rainbow trout is the state fish

**Metamorphosis:** a change from one form to another

Mayflies are a favorite food of trout. Trout rise to gobble the mayflies as they hatch into their flying, adult form.

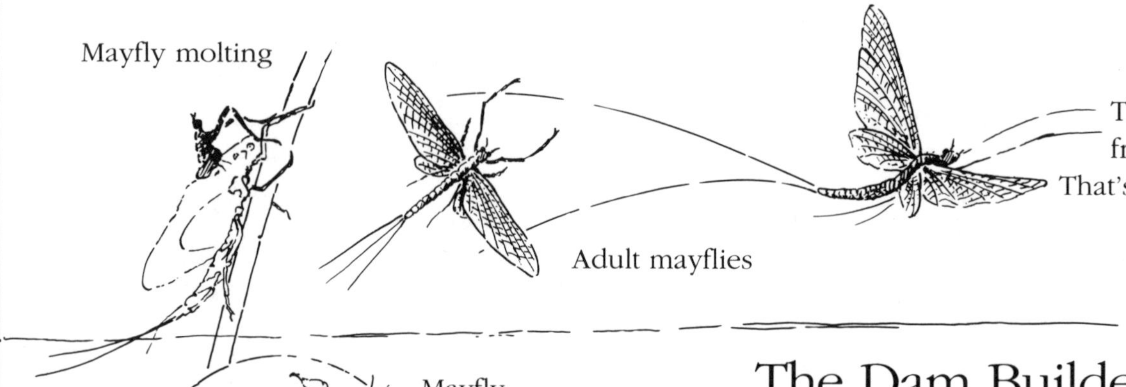

Mayfly molting

Adult mayflies

The mayfly changes from larva to adult. That's **metamorphosis**.

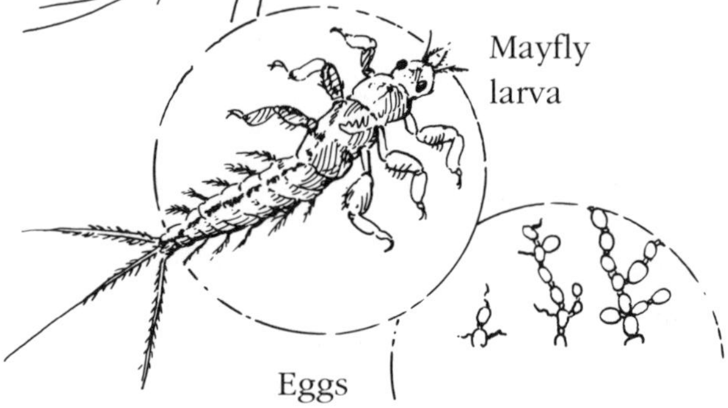

Mayfly larva

Eggs

## The Dam Builders

Some beavers live in ponds and lakes. Some beavers live in creeks and then turn them into ponds or lakes! Beavers change the habitat to suit their lifestyle.

Why do beavers turn creeks into ponds? Ponds make safe worlds for year-round living. Beavers can even eat tree bark underwater without swallowing water. That's because their lips close *behind* their gnawing front teeth!

## What a Tail!

*A prop for balance,*

*A store for fat,*

*A rudder for steering*

*And a warning, "Splat."*

Observe the trout at Boulder Creek Fish Observatory, Boulder (7).

City rivers are often polluted with oil, chemicals, fertilizers, and factory waste. No wonder wildlife doesn't care to live there any more!

A wildlife smile to people who bike or walk. That saves fuel and doesn't pollute.

# FANTASTIC FORESTS

Colorado has all kinds of forests. Some are dense and shady. Others are open and full of light. Each forest has its own kind of trees, flowers, mammals, and birds living in it.

**Check out a forest and record your finds. Circle the choice or fill in *your* observations.**

FOREST FINDS

| | | | |
|---|---|---|---|
| Forest is... | dense | sparse | open |
| Trees are... | evergreen | **deciduous** | both |
| Forest floor is... | ______ | ______ | ______ |
| Smells like... | ______ | ______ | ______ |
| I can hear... | ______ | ______ | ______ |
| Neatest thing is... | ______ | ______ | ______ |

Healthy forests are untidy. Standing dead trees, fallen tree trunks, and piles of brush wood make good homes for forest birds and mammals. Look for holes in snags (standing dead trees). They may be someone's door. Examine a fallen dead tree.

- What is the bark like?
- What kinds of tracks or footprints lead to the tree?
- Are there holes in the tree, or in the ground nearby? What do you think they are used for?
- Has anything been eating the tree? What?
- What is growing on the tree, or in its shelter?

## How Old?

Count rings on a cut tree to find its age. Rings close together show slow growing years, perhaps a drought. Rings wide apart show wetter growing seasons. The outer ring is the newest. If you have to cut a tree in your yard, write your family history on the stump or a slice of the tree.

**Deciduous:** trees that lose all their leaves in winter

Want to read more about it?
*Rocky Mountain Tree Finder.*
Tom Watts.
For tree names.

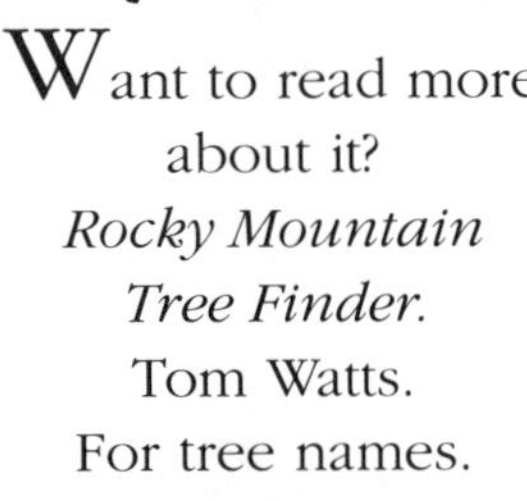

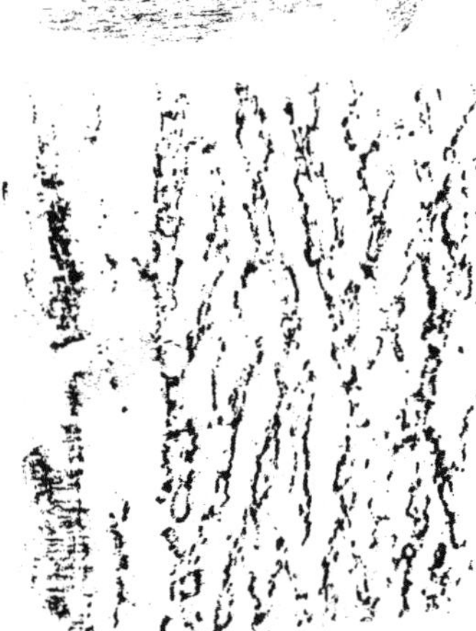

Ash

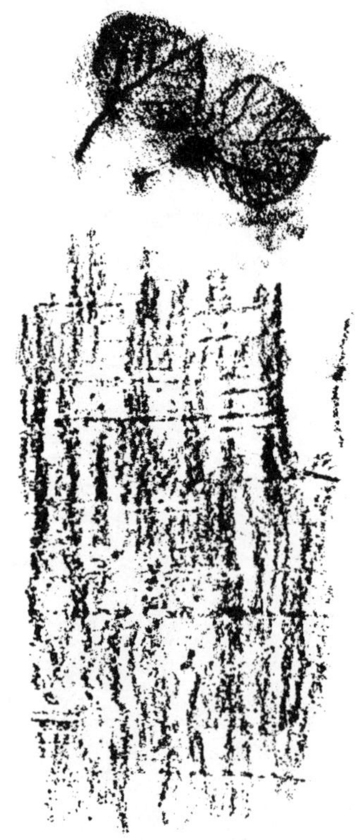

Aspen

# Tree Tributes

Make your own book of a special, favorite tree. Here are some ideas:

■ Make a bark rubbing.

■ Press leaves.

■ Draw spring, summer, fall, and winter pictures.

■ Hug your tree. Write about how it feels.

■ Write about how your tree smells.

■ Draw pictures, or write stories or poems, about the animals and birds in your tree.

■ Put in anything else you like about your tree.

Then, even when you can't visit your tree, you can read and think about it.

Black walnut

# Bark Rubbings

Use thin typing paper and a colored crayon, pastel, or charcoal. Hold the paper against the bark. Gently scribble over the whole paper to show the texture of the tree. Write the tree name on your rubbing if you know it, or can find out what it is. Start a collection of "take home tree trunks." Leaf and leaf-skeleton rubbings can be done in the same way.

# Aspen Gold

Fall. The aspen grove turns gold and reddish-gold. Why not save some gold for winter? Press the leaves between clear contact paper (or iron between wax paper) to make cards, bookmarks, and other treasures.

# Nifty Nest

Have you ever heard a tree cheeping? Maybe you heard hungry woodpecker chicks squawking for their lunch. They mistook your sounds for their parents coming with food!

Have you ever heard a tree hissing? Maybe you were hearing young woodpeckers mimicking (imitating) snakes to scare enemies away.

Piñon pine

# Forest Bingo!

Here are clues of natural things found in forests. How many can you find?
**Mark the ones you see—three in any row is FOREST BINGO!**

Ponderosa pine

Subalpine fir

# Why Needles?

Broad, flat leaves lose water fast in a dry climate. Thin needles with waxy surfaces don't dry out so fast in the heat, wind, and cold of Colorado. Conifers, with their needle-like leaves, save precious water this way.

# Piñon Nuts

*They're tasty treats for piñon jays,*
*A pack rat's store to last for days,*
*They're breakfast for a porcupine,*
*For bear and mule deer—great snack time.*

*For turkeys, tea. For chipmunks, lunch.*
*For nibbling squirrels—filling brunch.*
*Besides the creatures, people too,*
*Are nuts about piñon! How about you?*

Colorado blue spruce

Colorado State Flower is the columbine

Colorado State Tree is Colorado blue spruce

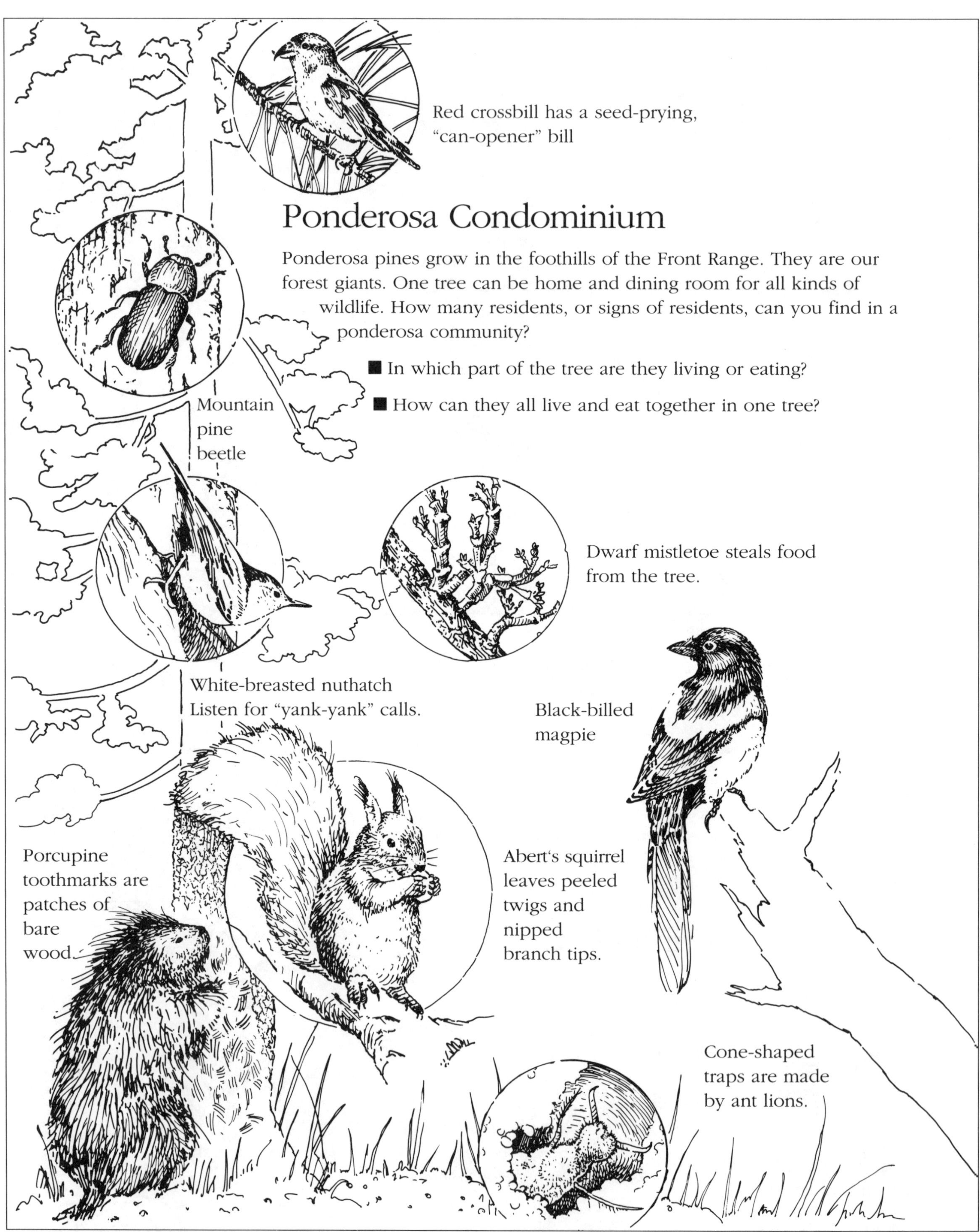


# Ponderosa Condominium

Ponderosa pines grow in the foothills of the Front Range. They are our forest giants. One tree can be home and dining room for all kinds of wildlife. How many residents, or signs of residents, can you find in a ponderosa community?

- In which part of the tree are they living or eating?
- How can they all live and eat together in one tree?

Check out a burn area. Check again in six months, two years, and many years. What changes can you see? Keep records in your journal.

## Forest on Fire!

Summer brings fierce thunderstorms to Colorado. Lightning cracks and flashes, often hitting forest trees, sometimes starting fires. Some trees have special adaptations to survive fire. Lodgepole pine is one of them.

- Collect lodgepole pine cones. (Collect only where it's allowed.)
- Place closed cones on aluminum foil in a warm oven (about 125°)—check often.
- How long does it take for the cones to open?
- Look for the seeds on the cone scales. Can you shake them out?
- Plant the seeds in pots of soil and give them tender, loving care.

Fire tidies up forests. It recycles dead trees and leaf litter. Ash from fires is full of nutrients. It helps get new plants off to a good start.

The first plants, the *pioneer* plants, grow from seeds released by the fire, or blown in from nearby. They thrive in bare, open places. As the years pass more plants arrive. Tree seedlings sprout and grow. Animals venture back to find food.

As the trees grow taller, they shade out wildflowers of the forest floor. The forest becomes dark and dense again—almost as it was before the fire. Different animals find food and shelter now. This chain of events is **succession.**

Look for signs of succession in other places that have been disturbed. Check out new road cuts, building sites, avalanche slides, and dried-up lakes. Succession is nature's way of starting over and healing scars.

Lodgepole pine cones open when fire melts the sap that kept the cones glued shut.

To see the effect of fire, hike to the Ouzel Burn in Wild Basin, Rocky Mountain National Park (5).

**Succession:** the changing plants and animals that live in a place as time passes

# Treks Above Timberline

Climb high enough in the mountains and the trees run out. The climate is too harsh. The trees can't survive the strong winds and long, cold winters.

## Elfin Timber

You may even be taller than the "elfin timber" at **timberline**. There trees struggle to survive in harsh winter winds and driving snow. Winds drive sharp ice crystals into the windward side of tree trunks, killing the tiny branches. With branches only on the sheltered side, the trees look like flags. Tree seedlings grow only in the shelter of rocks, fallen tree trunks, or already growing trees.

Check out a tree "island" at timberline:

- How far around is it? Count your steps.
- Can you crawl inside it?
- Can you find seedling trees?
- Can you find signs of animals?
- Can you see or hear birds?
- What do you like best about your tree island?

## Tundra

Above Colorado's timberline is the land called the alpine tundra. Tundra is not all the same. Places close to each other on the tundra have different microclimates (climates in tiny spaces). Some places have shelter, others have none. Sheltered spots keep their snow cover. Windy spots become dry and bare. Snow melts and water drains away in some areas. It stays to make bogs in other areas.

Elfin timber

**Timberline:** the boundary between trees and no trees that climate draws

Want to read more about it?
*Plants of the Alpine Tundra.*
Nic and Helen Marinos.
For more about cushion plants.

## Fragile Tundra

Tread softly on the tundra! A tiny cushion plant may be 25 years old. With such a short summer to grow in, plants struggle to survive, let alone add a millimeter to their size!

## Storms

You can't hide from storms on the tundra. The weather can change almost from one minute to the next. What begins as summer rain can quickly turn into a blizzard.

How can you be safe, exploring above tree line?

■ Hike early in the day. Thunderstorms usually start as the day warms up.

■ Get down into the shelter of the forests if you hear a storm coming. Don't shelter under the tallest trees.

■ If you are caught in the open, get off ridges. Squat down. Keep low so you will be safe from lightning strikes.

## Tundra Habitats

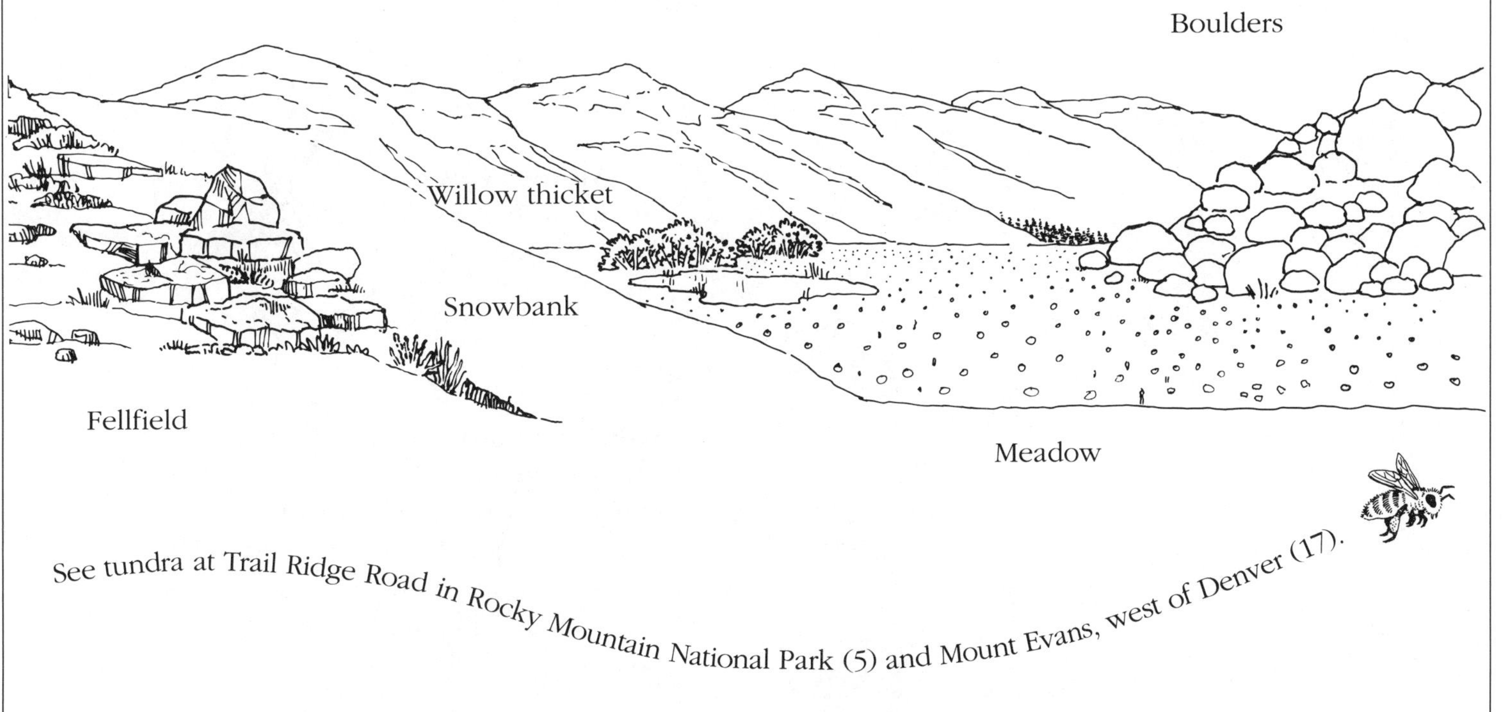


See tundra at Trail Ridge Road in Rocky Mountain National Park (5) and Mount Evans, west of Denver (17).

# Tundra Treasure Hunt

Check out different tundra habitats in your search of these animals, animal signs, and plants of the tundra. When you find one, color its picture so you have a record of the way it looked to you.

**Lichen**
Lichens are pioneers. They move into new, bare habitats.

**Phoebus parnassian**
White butterfly with red and black spots.

**Pika**
Listen for pika sounds. When do they call? Pikas clip meadow plants and store them under rocks for winter feasting. Look among rocks for a pika's haystack.

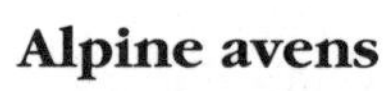

**Alpine avens**
Commonly grow in gopher gardens, where soil has been plowed.

**Yellow-bellied marmot**
Can you see why the yellow-bellied marmot got its name? Tundra marmots hibernate for seven or eight months of winter. They spend summer eating plants to build up their body fat. Watch them as they take time out to sunbathe.

**White-crowned sparrow**
Listen for the tuneful song of clear whistles and buzzy trills.

**Old-man-of-the-mountain**
Do you think his rays look like a halo? Which way does the old man face? Which insects come to sip nectar?

**Moss campion**
Moss campion grows in a tight cushion, low to the ground. That keeps the wind from harming the plant. If you could peek underground you'd see a long taproot. It reaches down to moisture and is a plant anchor too.

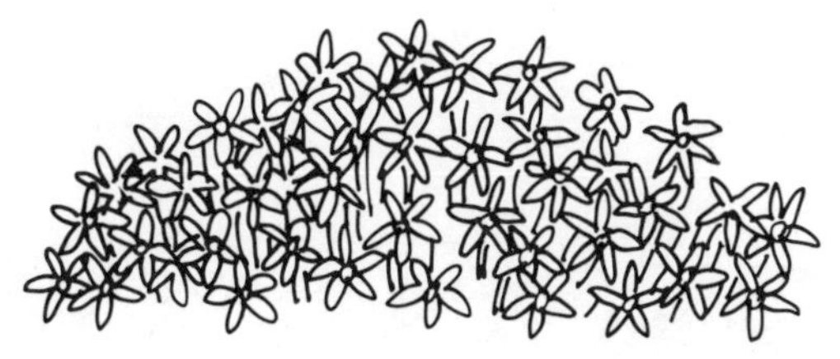

**White-tailed ptarmigan**
Look for these birds winter or summer—no migrating to Mexico for them! Survival clues: feathered, snowshoe feet, winter-white feathers, bud-pecking bills, and rock-gray summer disguises.

**Alpine forget-me-not**
Alpine forget-me-nots have tiny flowers as blue as the Colorado sky. Look at the tiny leaves. They have a feature that helps them save water: they are hairy.

# EAT OR BE EATEN

Every animal must eat to stay alive. It can't breathe or move, grow or have babies, without energy from food. Only plants can use the sun's energy to make food. Animals get the sun's energy secondhand from plants.

Lots of grass feeds one grasshopper.

Lots of grasshoppers feed one frog.

Lots of frogs feed one bullsnake.

There could NEVER be as many bullsnakes as there are blades of grass. Nature doesn't work that way.

Animals can be **predators** *and* **prey**. A robin is a predator when it eats an earthworm. The robin is prey if a Cooper's hawk swoops down and gobbles it up.

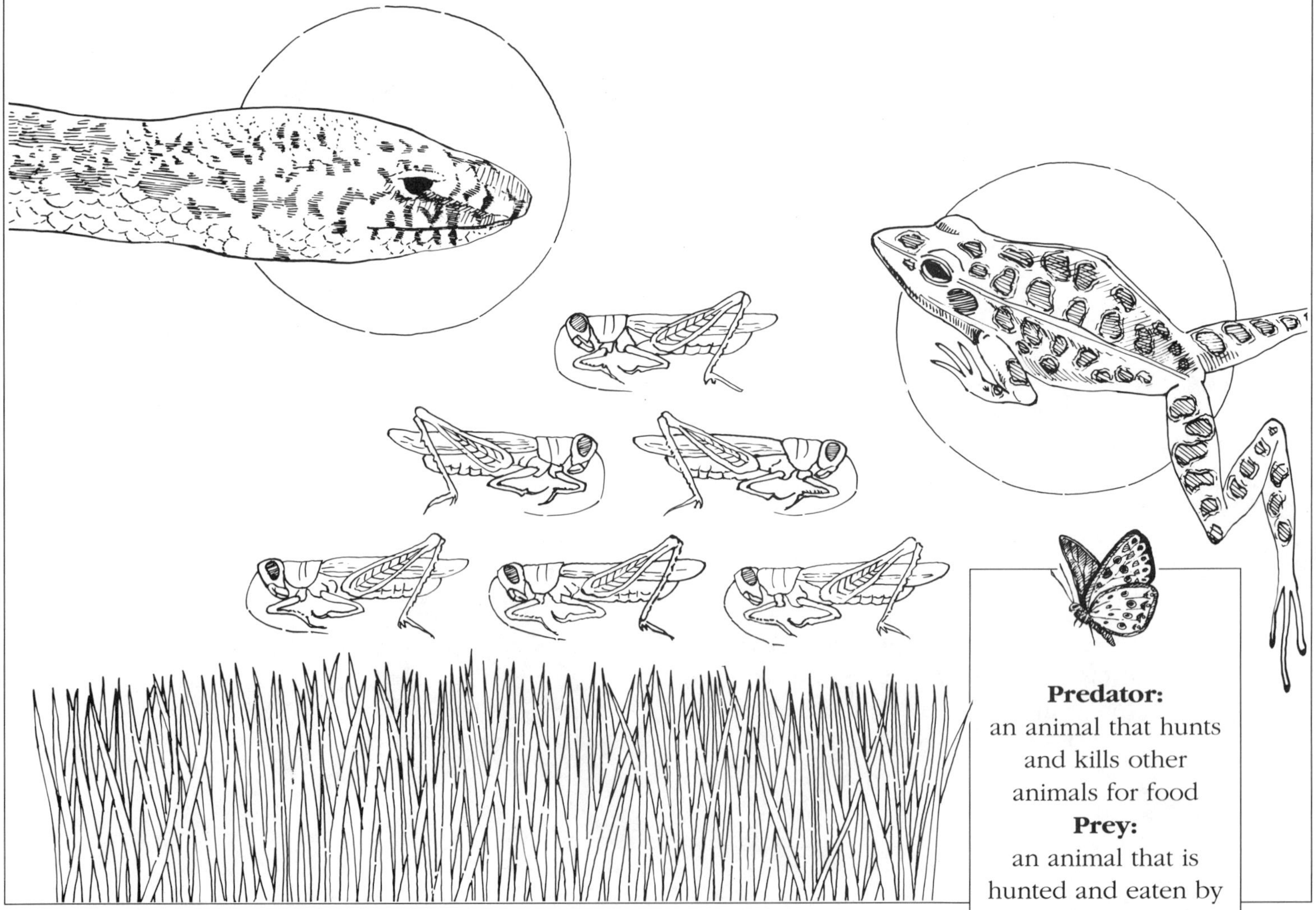

**Predator:**
an animal that hunts and kills other animals for food
**Prey:**
an animal that is hunted and eaten by another animal

What other ways do animals catch their prey? Start a special "tools for the hunt" page in your journal.

## Big and Little

Predators are not all large, fierce animals. They come in all sizes.

Mountain lions hunt by night and rest by day. They catch and eat many kinds of prey. Mule deer, elk, bighorn sheep, beaver, and rabbits may all be on the menu. These big cats will even eat porcupine—if that's all they can get!

Pygmy shrews are fierce predators, too. These tiny mammals hunt day and night, summer and winter. They must eat almost constantly to keep warm and active—their diet includes insects and worms.

Pygmy shrew life size!

Believe it or not:

- A pygmy shrew can hunt along an earthworm burrow.
- Shrews nap between frantic food forays.
- Shrews eat their own weight, or more, of food each day. (That's like a person eating two or three *hundred* hamburgers in a day!)

## Tools for the Hunt

Look for these kinds of tools for the hunt when you wildwatch:

- sharp canine teeth (like a coyote) for catching prey,
- claws for digging into prairie dog holes, like a badger,
- fangs with poison, like the prairie rattlesnake,
- talons to grip a jackrabbit, like a golden eagle.

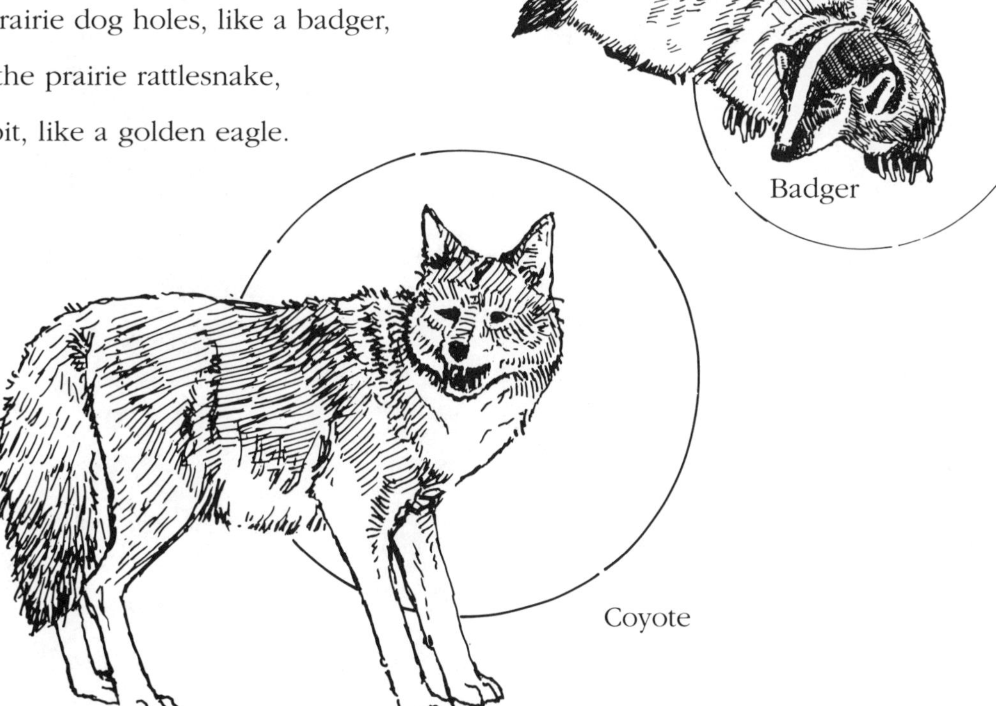

Badger

Coyote

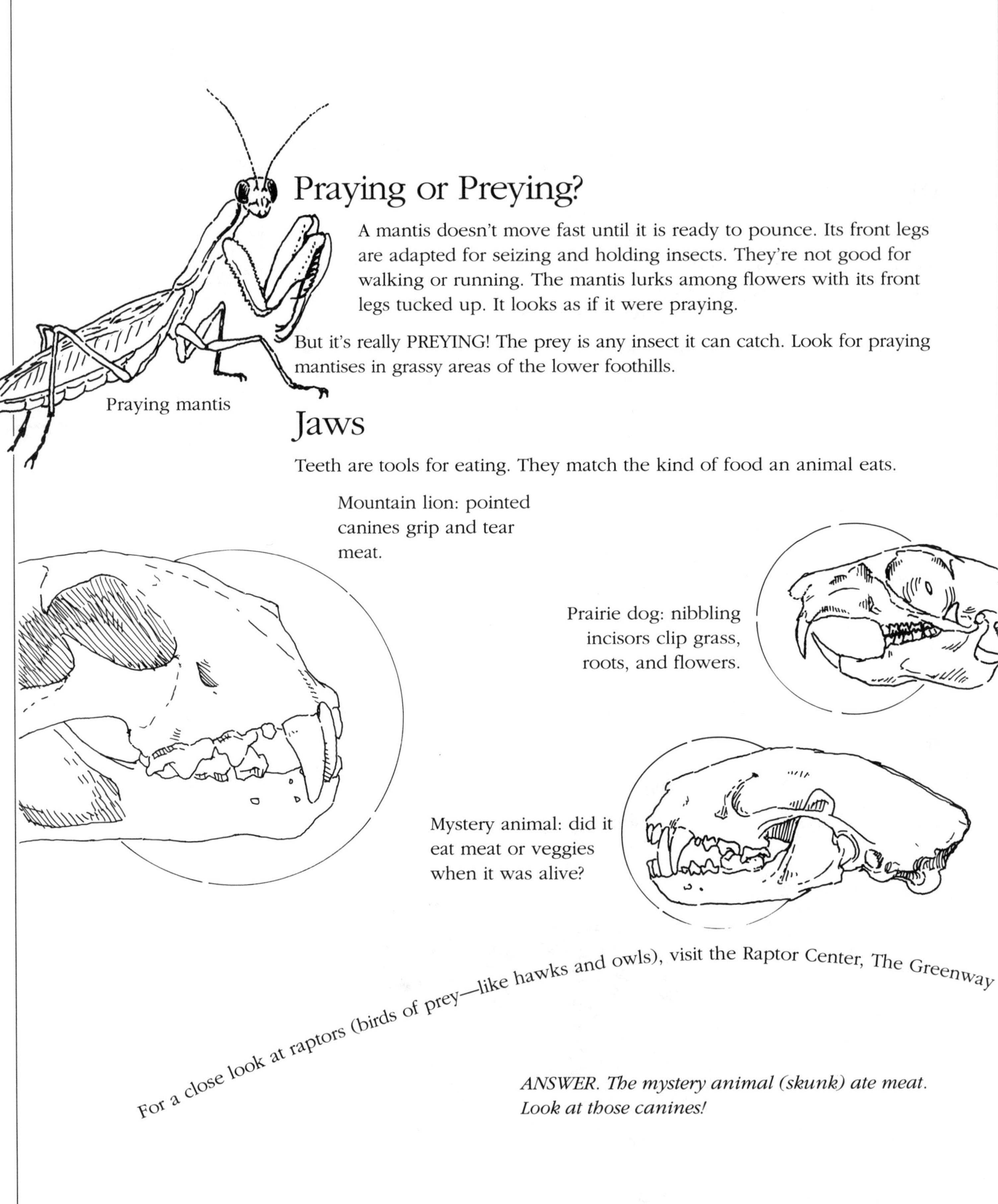

## Praying or Preying?

A mantis doesn't move fast until it is ready to pounce. Its front legs are adapted for seizing and holding insects. They're not good for walking or running. The mantis lurks among flowers with its front legs tucked up. It looks as if it were praying.

But it's really PREYING! The prey is any insect it can catch. Look for praying mantises in grassy areas of the lower foothills.

Praying mantis

## Jaws

Teeth are tools for eating. They match the kind of food an animal eats.

Mountain lion: pointed canines grip and tear meat.

Prairie dog: nibbling incisors clip grass, roots, and flowers.

Mystery animal: did it eat meat or veggies when it was alive?

For a close look at raptors (birds of prey—like hawks and owls), visit the Raptor Center, The Greenway

*ANSWER. The mystery animal (skunk) ate meat. Look at those canines!*

## Predator Plants?

Plants don't hunt and kill animals for food, except in science fiction stories...or do they?

Bladderwort, a pond plant with small balloon floats, can suck up tiny water insects like a miniature vacuum cleaner. The plant is a meat-eater—a carnivore! It eats meat for the extra nutrition.

Bladderwort

## Create a Predator

If you could design a predator, what would it look like? How would it catch its prey? What would it eat? Imagine. . .

Would it have:

- Sharp eyesight?
- Keen hearing?
- Sense of smell?
- A special way of getting about?
- Tools for the hunt?
- A disguise?
- Anything else to help it survive?

**Draw your own predator here.**

and Nature Center of Pueblo (25).

# NOBODY WANTS TO BE DINNER

Animals try to keep safe from their enemies. Nobody wants to be a predator's dinner! Some animals run or fly to safety. Others pop into their holes. Their safety lies in hiding. These animals stop what they are doing to run or hide. That takes time away from eating, home building, or other jobs on hand.

How can animals be safer while getting on with their busy lives? One way is to blend in with their surroundings. **Camouflage** works for prey and predator alike. It hides prey from its enemies. It hides a predator as it sneaks up on its prey or lurks in ambush.

Hairstreak butterfly

## Crab Camouflage

A crab spider doesn't spin a web to catch food like most spiders. It lurks in flowers, ready to pounce on unwary insects. Its bright yellow body matches the yellow flowers on which it lives. Check out sunflowers along roadsides, open fields or meadows, vacant lots, or in your own garden. These are good crab spider hideouts.

Check out white daisies, too. Are there any spiders lying in wait? What color are they?

## Bluffers

Some animals bluff their way to safety. They are "con artists" by instinct.

- A hairstreak butterfly has wing-tails that look like antennae. It is hard to know which way it will fly.
- A hognosed snake flips on its back and plays dead. Flip it on its front and it will wriggle over and play dead again!
- The wood nymph has fake eyes in the wings. If a bird pecks at those eyes, the butterfly can still fly away, tattered but safe.
- A click beetle sees with tiny eyes and large, fake eyes to warn.

Hognosed snake

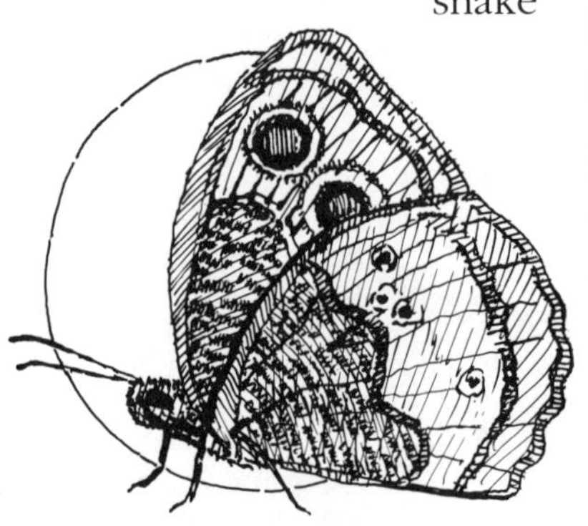

Wood nymph

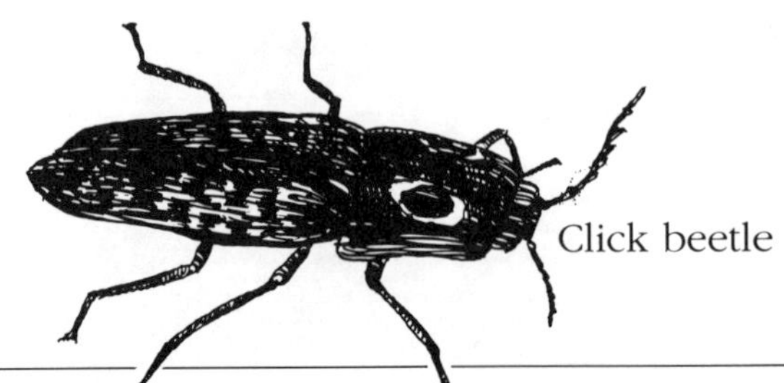

Click beetle

**Camouflage:** color or shape that helps to conceal

# Hidden Animals

**Try to find eight animals hidden in this picture.**

- ❑ Screech owl. Matches tree trunk on which it snoozes.
- ❑ Small-eyed sphinx moth. Looks as if it were made of bark.
- ❑ Fence lizard. Mottled like rock lichens.
- ❑ Walkingstick. Looks like stem of grass until it crawls away!
- ❑ Hairstreak butterfly. Lands with closed wings lined up with the sun, so its shadow is narrow.
- ❑ Treehoppers. Shaped like thorns.
- ❑ Mule deer fawn. Dappled, like sun speckling through leaves.
- ❑ Chipmunk. Stripes disguise the eyes.

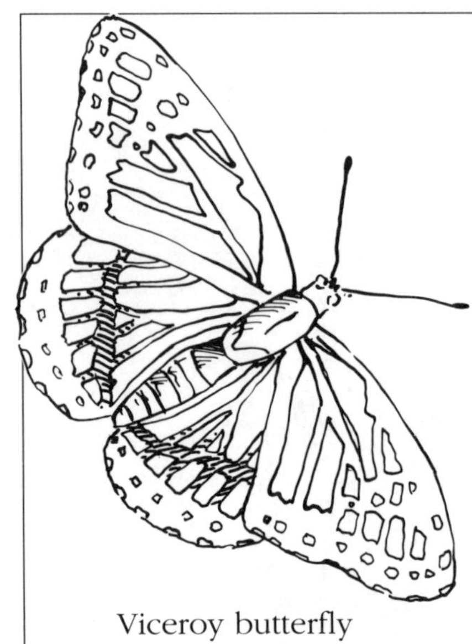

Viceroy butterfly

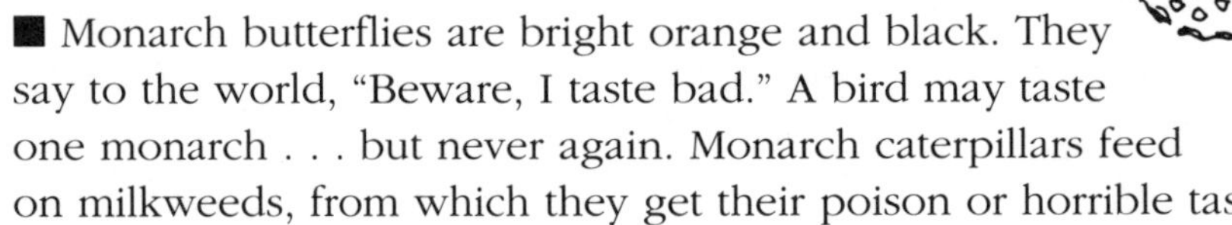

Monarch butterfly

## It Pays to Advertise

What about brightly colored animals? They seem to be safe in spite of being easy to see. What is their secret?

■ Monarch butterflies are bright orange and black. They say to the world, "Beware, I taste bad." A bird may taste one monarch . . . but never again. Monarch caterpillars feed on milkweeds, from which they get their poison or horrible taste.

■ Ladybugs advertise in black and red. "Keep off, bad taste."

■ Wasps are armed with a stinger. They give their warning in yellow and black. "Don't mess with me."

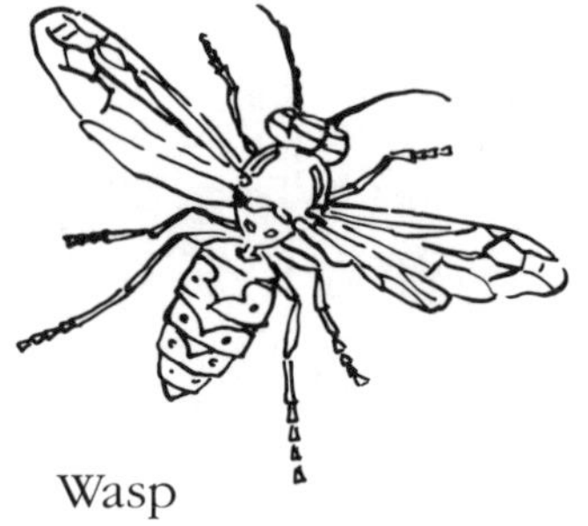

Wasp

## Copycat Creatures

Some animals are not poisonous or bad tasting, but they look like animals that are. It is like false advertising. They have bright colors. Predators think they are poisonous and leave them alone.

■ An orange and black viceroy looks like a monarch. Can you spot the difference? Most birds can't.

■ Black-and-yellow wasp-copycats don't sting. Flies, beetles, and moths are often mistaken for wasps and left alone. It doesn't always work.

Wasp mimic fly

Wasp mimic moth

Ladybug

# The Clean-Up Crew

Who tidies up nature? Who buries dead animals? Who sweeps away fallen leaves? Who keeps ponds clean? Scavengers and decomposers—that's who! They are nature's recyclers—the clean-up crew. Without them:

- no new soil would be made,
- chemicals that are important for life would not be recycled,
- we'd be buried in leaves (or carcasses) ourselves!

Look for these decomposers (or "recyclers"):

- Earthworms digest leaves. Their castings make rich soil.
- Each millipede species has its favorite kind of dead leaves.
- A burying beetle lays eggs in a small animal carcass that it buries by digging soil out from beneath the body.
- Watch snails clean algae off the sides of an aquarium tank.

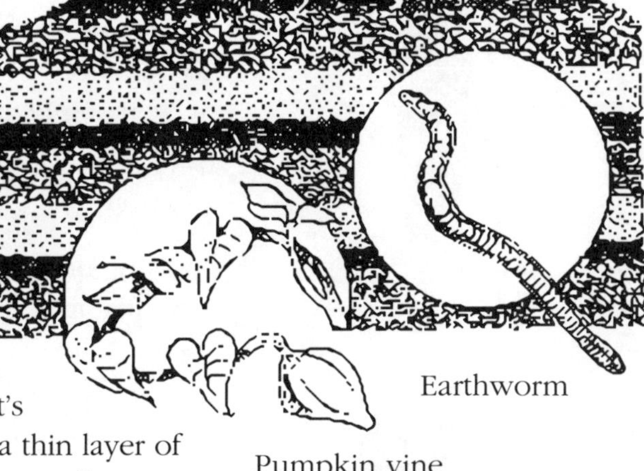


## Abracadabra Soil!

Don't throw away kitchen scraps! Your garbage could be someone's dinner. Build a compost pile on the ground, or in a garbage bag or bin. Start with a layer of organic matter—that's leaves, grass clippings, kitchen scraps, or weeds. Next put on a thin layer of soil. Top with some manure. Keep building up these layers. Wet well.

Tiny scavengers and decomposers in the soil will get busy. Your garbage is their food. Over the months—abracadabra—they change garbage into rich, black soil, or humus. Plant pumpkin seeds in this humus. They will grow well in this magic mixture.

## Body to Bones

If you find a dead bird or small mammal, cover it with wire mesh. Peg the mesh down so no large scavengers can carry off your experiment. Check each day to see who is feasting and what is happening to the body. How long does it take to go from body to bones?

NOTE: Always wash your hands well if you touch a dead animal.

A wildlife smile to people who recycle. Are you one of them?

Recycle newspaper—save energy and trees.

Recycle aluminum—save energy and minerals.

Recycle glass—save energy and space in landfills.

## Beetle Booby Trap

Sink a coffee can into the earth so its rim is level with the ground. Prop a flat rock or plank a few inches above the can. It will keep out rain. Bait your booby trap with meat, cheese, or fish—something smelly! Next morning you should find beetles who were prowling for dead animals in the night. After you have studied them, let them go quickly into the dark of the leaf litter. They are nocturnal. They don't like the bright light and heat of day. Try your trap in different places.

## Beetlemania

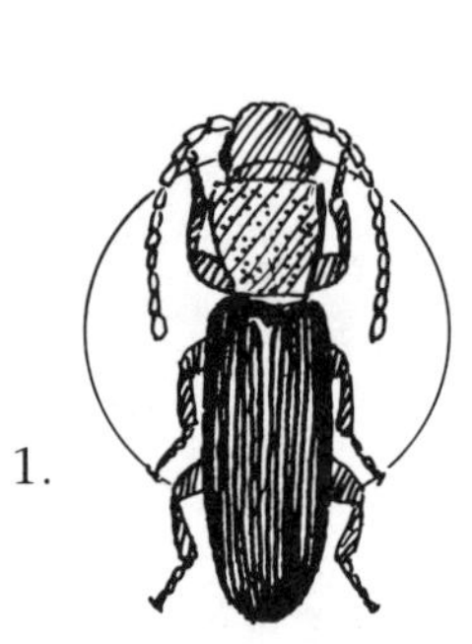

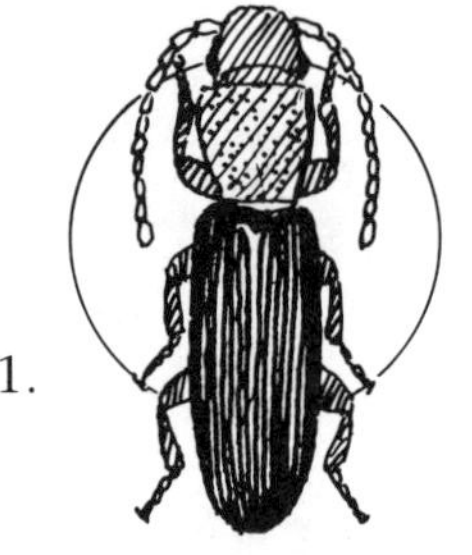

1.

It is hard NOT to find beetles, there are so many of them. Scientists have found about 24,000 different kinds in this country. Here are some scavenging beetles to look out for as you wildwatch.

1. Bark beetle. Attacks dead or dying trees, making complicated tunnels under the bark.

2. Dung beetle. Rolls a ball of dung away to bury in the ground. But not until a single egg has been laid in it. Dung is food for the larva when it hatches.

3. Hide beetle. Feeds on animal hair, hides, feathers, and even fur coats and sweaters. Don't say PEST, say RECYCLER!

4. Whirligig beetle. Scavenges dead animals and plants in the pond. Has two pairs of compound eyes, one pair for underwater and one pair for above the surface.

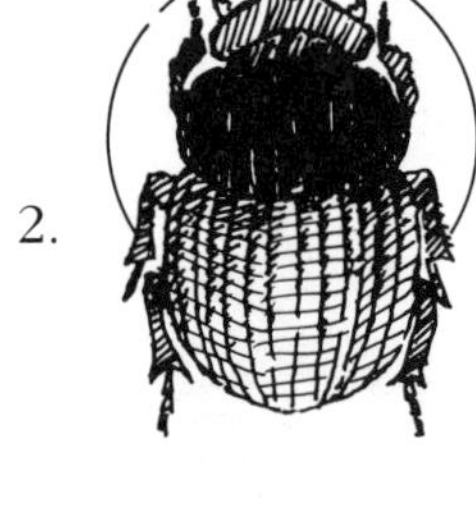

2.

*Compound* eyes are made of lots of little eyes close together. Each tiny eye sees an image. The whole compound eye sees a whole scene in dots.

3.

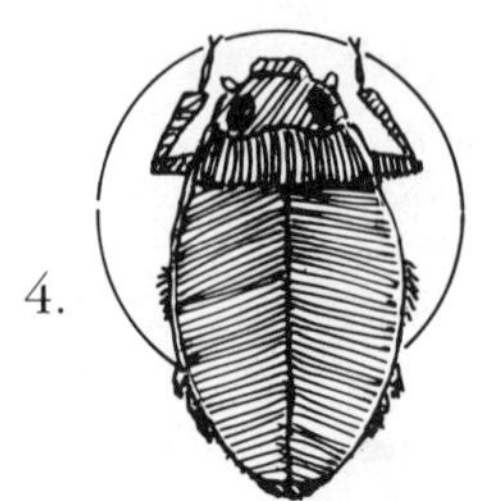

4.

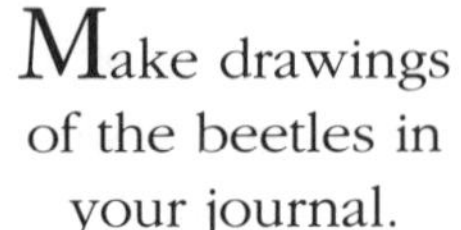

Make drawings of the beetles in your journal.

# Day and Night Wildlife

## Let's Go Prowling!

Invite a grown-up to go wildwatching with you after dark and see what you can see, hear, smell, and feel! Spooky?

Good places to prowl:

- a backyard
- a campsite
- a riverbank
- a swamp or pond
- a brightly lit place in the city

Before you go night-walking let your eyes get used to the dark. It takes about half an hour to adapt to darkness. Use a flashlight covered in red plastic. Most night animals can't see red, but your eyes can see the night creatures in the red light.

- What sounds can you hear? Squeaking? Snuffling? Croaking?
- How good is your sense of body-space? Can you feel when you are close to trees? On a worn path?
- What night-fliers are seeking bright lights?
- Is anyone watching you? Check for eyeshine with your flashlight. Light reflects off the mirror-like backs of some animals' eyes.
- Many birds migrate at night. They save the days to forage or food. Try counting birds as you see their dark shapes against a full moon.

**Competition:** two kinds of living things trying to use the same resource

# Day Shift–Night Shift

Red-tailed hawks and great horned owls are predators. They both catch small birds and rodents. They would be in **competition** if they hunted at the same time. How do they avoid competition? Hawks take the day shift. Owls take the night shift.

■ Red-tailed hawks hunt by sight. Their forward-facing eyes judge distance well. This is important for a hunter swooping on a tiny vole.

■ Great horned owls have good night vision. They also have sensitive ears to judge the location of a scampering deer mouse.

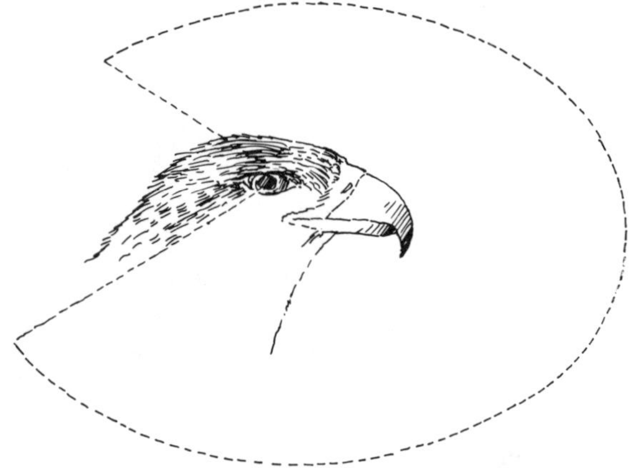

The owl turns its head to see sideways (and behind).

The hawk sees well without turning its head–up to a mile!

# Which Shift?

Many animals eat insects. To make sure that all animals get enough of what they need, they avoid competition in two ways.

■ They choose different kinds of insects than other animals hunting at the same time.

■ They hunt the same insects, but at different times or places.

**Sort these competitors into Day-shift (D) or Night-shift (N) (and dusk shift!)**

| | | |
|---|---|---|
| ___ Bat | ___ Dragonfly | ___ Swallow |
| ___ Chickadee | ___ Nighthawk | ___ Robin |
| ___ Lizard | ___ Wolf spider | ___ Frog |

*ANSWERS: Day-shift: Dragonfly, Swallow, Chickadee, Robin, Lizard.*
*Night-shift: Bat, Nighthawk, Wolf spider.*
*Both shifts: Nighthawk, Frog*

**Diurnal:**
active during the day
**Nocturnal:**
active during the night

Some animals are **diurnal**. They search for food by day. Predators can easily see them. They have to be quick to escape becoming dinner!

■ Painted turtles moves fast to feed or escape in the warmth of the day.

■ Barn swallows use good eyes to catch insects on the wing.

■ Meadow voles scurry through grassy tunnels finding seeds.

Barn swallow

Some animals are **nocturnal**. They search for food at night. They may have special eyes to help them see. They may have sharp hearing. They may hunt by smell. Darkness becomes their blanket of safety.

■ Deer mice search for seeds in darkness.

■ Great horned owls hunt mice and small birds with night vision eyes and sensitive ears.

■ Prairie rattlesnakes track mice by sensing their body warmth.

■ Slugs feed in the cool damp of night.

People are diurnal animals. We see signs of animals who are active at dusk, at dawn, or at night. But we don't get to meet the animals unless we join them in the hours of darkness.

Great horned owl

## Blind as a Bat?

Colorado's bats are nighttime hunters. They catch insects as they skim through the air at dusk. They are not blind, but they do not have keen vision. Instead they use *echolocation* to find their prey.

Bats squeak as they fly. You may be able to hear them. The high-pitched squeaks bounce back as echoes when they hit a solid object. By listening to the echoes the bats avoid bumping into things as they fly. They also catch enough moths, beetles, and mosquitoes for a meal.

## Weird Wonder

Some moths squeak like bats! The squeaks are to confuse the bats so the moths can escape.

## Moth Marvels

Butterflies are easy to see, especially if you have colorful nectar flowers in your garden. Butterflies are active in the warmth of day.

Moths are harder to find. They fly at night and find nectar in night-blooming flowers. They find moth-mates by scent. The female moths have special smelly chemicals, called pheromones, to attract the males.

Moths are attracted to bright lights. Pin an old white sheet against the side of your house or on a fence and shine a strong flashlight at it. This attracts moths that you can study against the white background.

Look for:

❏ feathery antennae

❏ furry bodies

❏ colorful hind wings when the moth lands with both pairs of wings spread. Look for night-fliers anywhere there are bright lights—from porches to ballparks.

## Fireflies in Colorado?

Look in damp places—river valleys, ponds, and swamps—for the telltale flashing of fireflies. They flash signals to each other on summer evenings. Chemicals in the abdomen act like tiny lanterns that flash on and off. It's a special code that other fireflies of the same kind recognize. Males keep other males away with the flashing and try to find females with which to mate.

Fireflies in Colorado are a rare find!

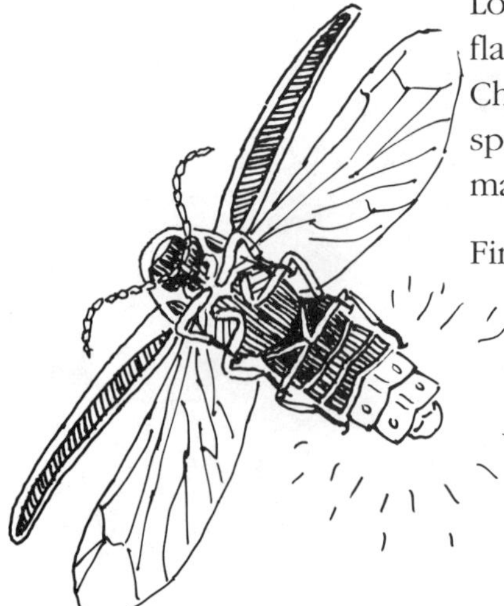

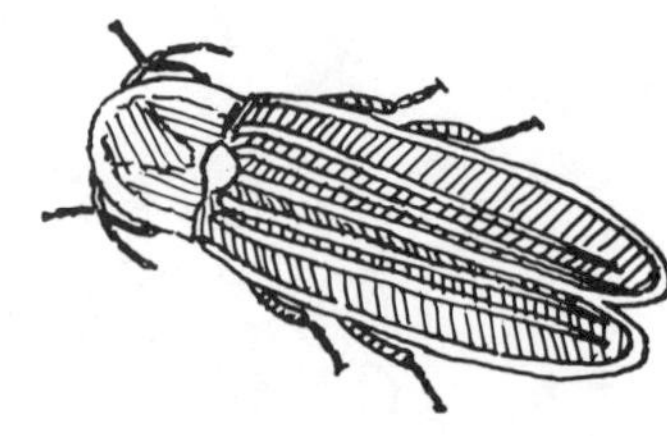

# CRAWLY CREATURES

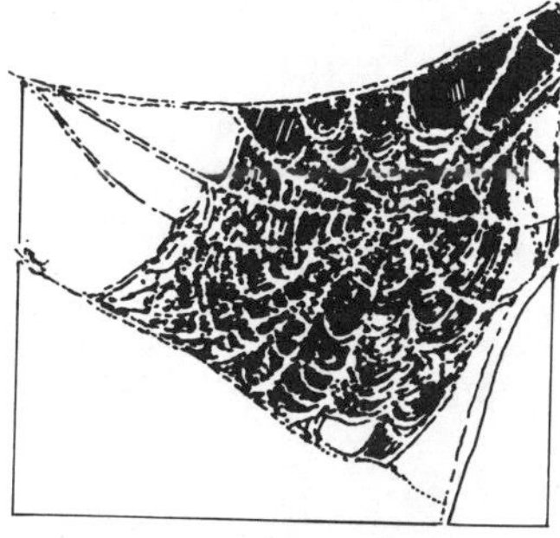

## Who Lives with You?

You don't need to go places to wildwatch for insects, spiders, and other smally-crawlies. They share your home, inside and out.

Check cracks, corners, windowsills, washbasins, woodpiles, leaves, log bottoms, lighting fixtures. Be careful! Don't touch. Just watch until you know you haven't found a poisonous kind—ask a grown-up. Are you surprised how many animals share your home?

To see more insect night life, shine a bright light in your window in summer. Moths, lacewings, midges, mosquitoes, and even beetles will crawl against the window. Look at their undersides, legs, and antennae as they try to get to your light.

## Watched by a Thousand Eyes!

Open an umbrella and hang it upside down from a branch of a tree. Or spread an old sheet underneath a bush. Shake the leaves and branches hard, but without breaking them. How many eyes were watching you?

## Bugarium

Make a bugarium to keep your insect finds in while you study them. You can watch while they carry on their lives.

**You'll need:**

- 2 round cake pans or two large lids
- a piece of old window screen
- a margarine tub with lid

Set up as shown. Bend the screen edges for strength. Fill the tub with water to keep the leaves fresh.

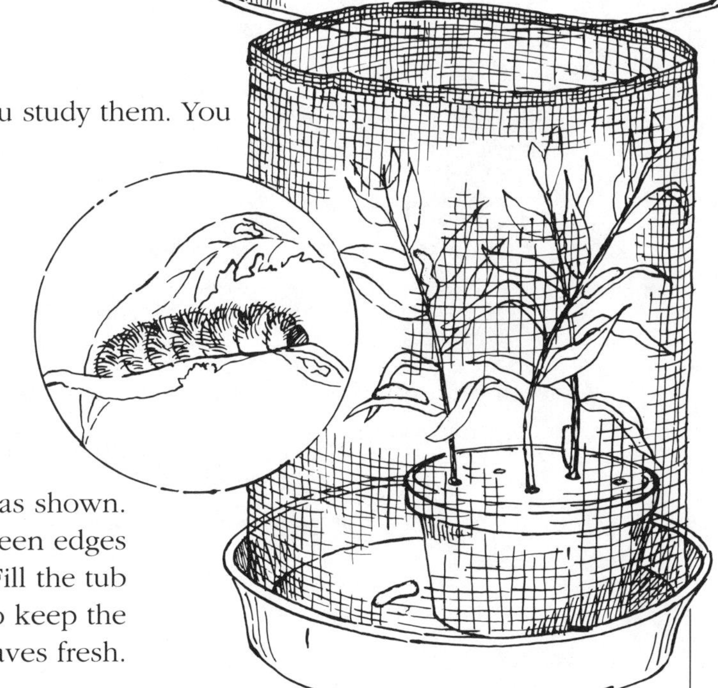

Look at your catch with a magnifying glass. Draw pictures of your finds before you let them all go again.

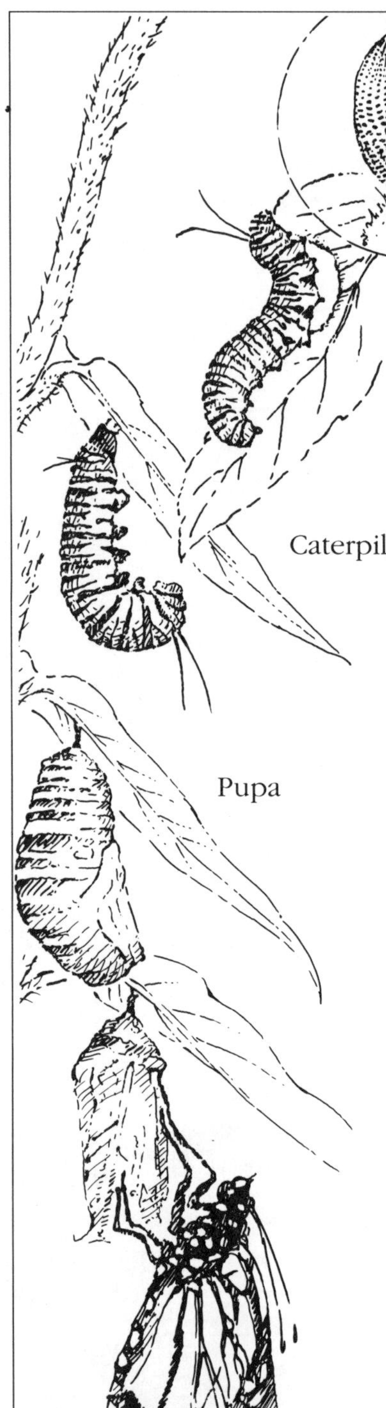

Monarch butterfly

Find caterpillars with a piece of branch they are feeding on. Supply fresh leaves of the right kind each day. You can keep the caterpillars until they pupate. A butterfly caterpillar turns into a pupa. A moth caterpillar spins itself a cocoon. Watch for them to hatch. What did your larvae become? Let your finds go again at the end of your studies. They need to carry on their lives.

## Spider Search

Every spider has a different way of catching a meal. Stay-at-home spiders wait for their prey to come to them. Hunting spiders actively search for their prey.

- An orb weaver spins beautiful round webs with silk from her spinnerets. Some silken strands are sticky. Watch out, prey!
- A wolf spider hunts at night and even takes her eggs and later her babies with her on the hunt.
- A trap-door spider lurks in a neat silk-lined burrow beneath a close-fitting lid.

## Catch a Web

After a shower, or on a dewy morning, every spider's web sparkles with silvery, liquid beads. You don't have to wait for natural moisture. Find a web and ornament it with imitation rain.

**You'll need:**

- a spray bottle full of water

Spray the web gently from a distance of about twelve inches. Each delicate strand of lacy "tablecloth" will be outlined with crystal droplets. You'll see the details of a beautiful weaving job. And if the spider happens to get an unexpected bath, she'll come to no harm!

How strong is spider silk? You'd be surprised. Ounce for ounce it's stronger than steel. Find a strand of silk. Can you hang a pencil from it?

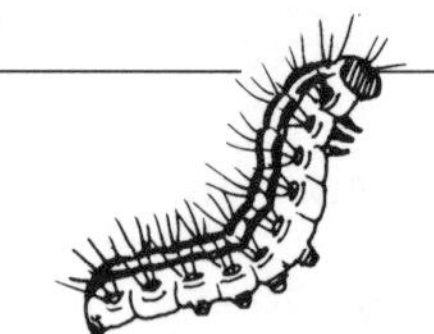

Want to read more about it?
*Familiar Insects and Spiders.*
John Farrand.
For good pictures.
*An Instant Guide to Insects,*
by Pamela Forey.
For quick information on insect groups.

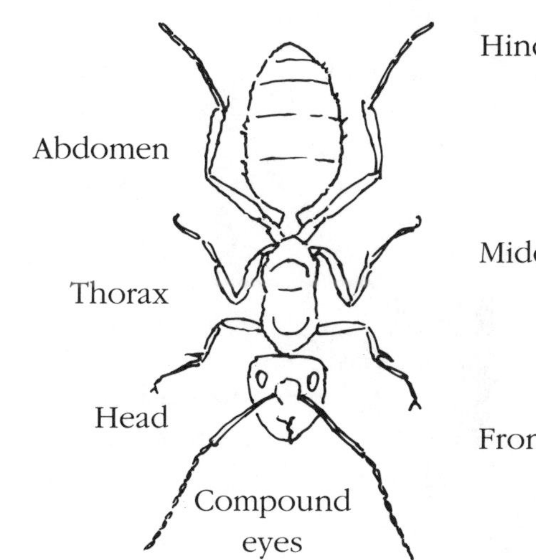


# Is It an Insect?

**Circle the insects. Not sure? Ask yourself these questions:**

- How many legs does it have?
- What kind of eyes does it have?
- Does it have antennae?
- How many body parts does it have?

If you answer six legs, compound eyes, antennae, and three body parts—it's an insect! Remember, compound eyes are made of lots of little eyes close together. Each tiny eye sees an image. The whole compound eye sees a whole scene in dots.

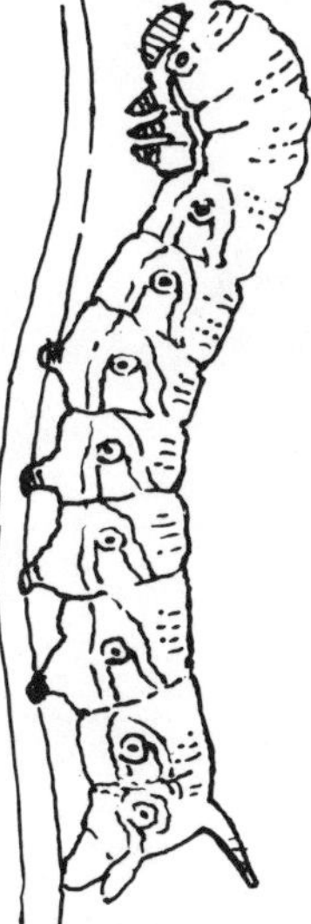

Tomato hornworm larva

Is this an insect? You can't use the "Is It an Insect?" test! Some insects don't show those insect features until they are grown up. The larvae may be so different from the adults that you'd think they were different kinds of animals. How can you know they belong together? House and feed the larvae in your bugarium until transformation time.

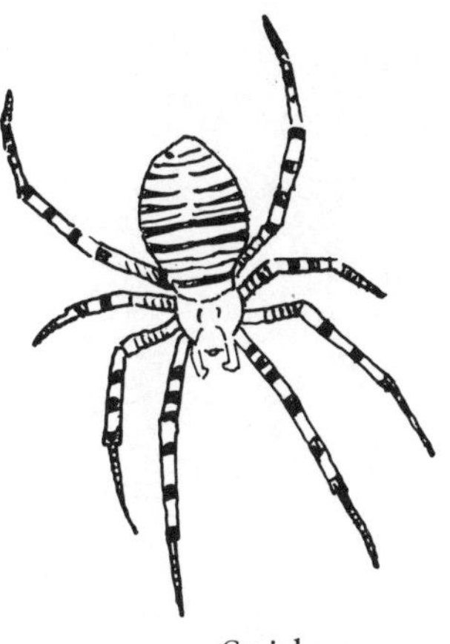

Spider

Many crawly creatures you find are not insects. They are like insects in some ways, but different in other ways. They all belong together in a group scientists call *arthropods* (jointed-legged animals).

Spiders have eight legs, simple eyes, two body parts, and usually no antennae. A simple eye has one lens. It sees one image.

Centipedes have many body segments, many legs, and tiny eyes.

Centipede

Grasshopper

Observe insects and other arthropods at University of Colorado Museum, Boulder (9).

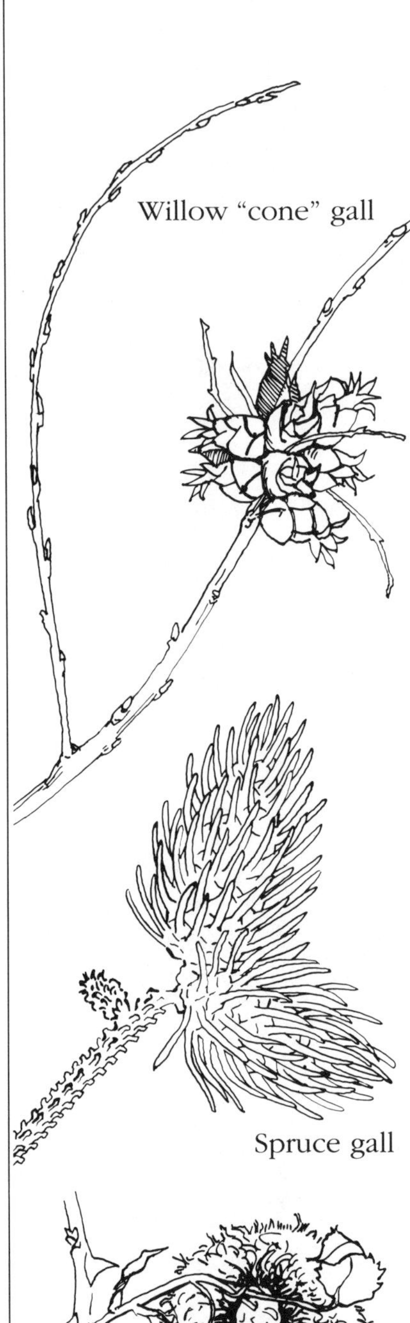


## Galls

These strange bumps and lumps on plants are galls. The plant tissue grows the gall when an insect mother lays an egg in the plant stem or leaf. The insect larva, safely hidden, munches the inside of its home. It emerges when it is grown to start the cycle again. Each kind of gall belongs to a different kind of insect.

- A willow "cone" gall is made by a gnat.
- A spruce gall is made by an aphid.
- A "Robin's pincushion" is made by a gall wasp.

## Buggy Puzzlers

Now that you're an experienced insect watcher, can you complete this challenge?

- What part of a grasshopper makes noise?
- How many wings does a damselfly have?
- How many wings does a house fly have?
- Do all butterflies perch in the same way?
- Do moths rest in the same way as butterflies?
- Do moths and butterflies have the same kind of antennae?

Watch the massing ladybugs on Green Mountain in Boulder Mountain Parks (8). Ladybird beetles migrate to

"Robin's pincushion" on rose plant

*ANSWERS:*
*1. Noise is from one body part rubbing another, wings against legs, or wings against wings.*
*2. A damselfly has four wings (two pairs).*
*3. A house fly has two flying wings and two tiny wing buds.*
*4. Some butterflies land flat-winged, others close their wings above them.*
*5. Moths usually rest with wings folded over their backs.*
*6. Moths usually have feathery antennae. Butterfly antennae are club-like.*

# Ladybug Fly Home

*One*

*and*

*Two*

*Come*

*Flying*

*Through.*

*Three and Four*

*Then more and more.*

*A swirling flame*

*Against the gray*

*As beetle ribbons*

*Make their way*

*Above the trees*

*To hilltop high*

*So bleak and cold*

*In snow-flecked sky.*

*The beetle armies*

*All will stop*

*In cracks and crannies*

*At the top.*

*The time for winter sleep has come.*

*The ladybugs are flying home.*

the summit and hibernate in rock crevices and under tree bark.

# Happy Families

Every animal must have a home. Go on a wildlife house tour. You'll be amazed at the variety of building styles.

■ House sparrows construct untidy nests of straw and plant stems. Townhouse sites include stoplights and store signs.

■ Harvester ants build ant cities and share the work between them.

■ Yellow-headed blackbirds weave nests on cattail scaffolds that blow in the breeze.

■ Barn swallows use saliva-glue to stick their mud-pellet nests under a bridge.

■ Spittle-bug larvae live in foam homes. They're made from air bubbled into plant juices that are excreted by the larvae.

■ Tent caterpillars camp out in their web-tents and are often found on chokecherry and wild plum bushes.

Tent caterpillars

## Oo-Ahh! How Cute!

Spring is the time to see fluffy yellow goslings, tiny rabbits, and other growing families. They're cute, but they're wild. They don't make good pets. Even if you don't see an animal parent nearby, leave the babies alone! Mother will be back!

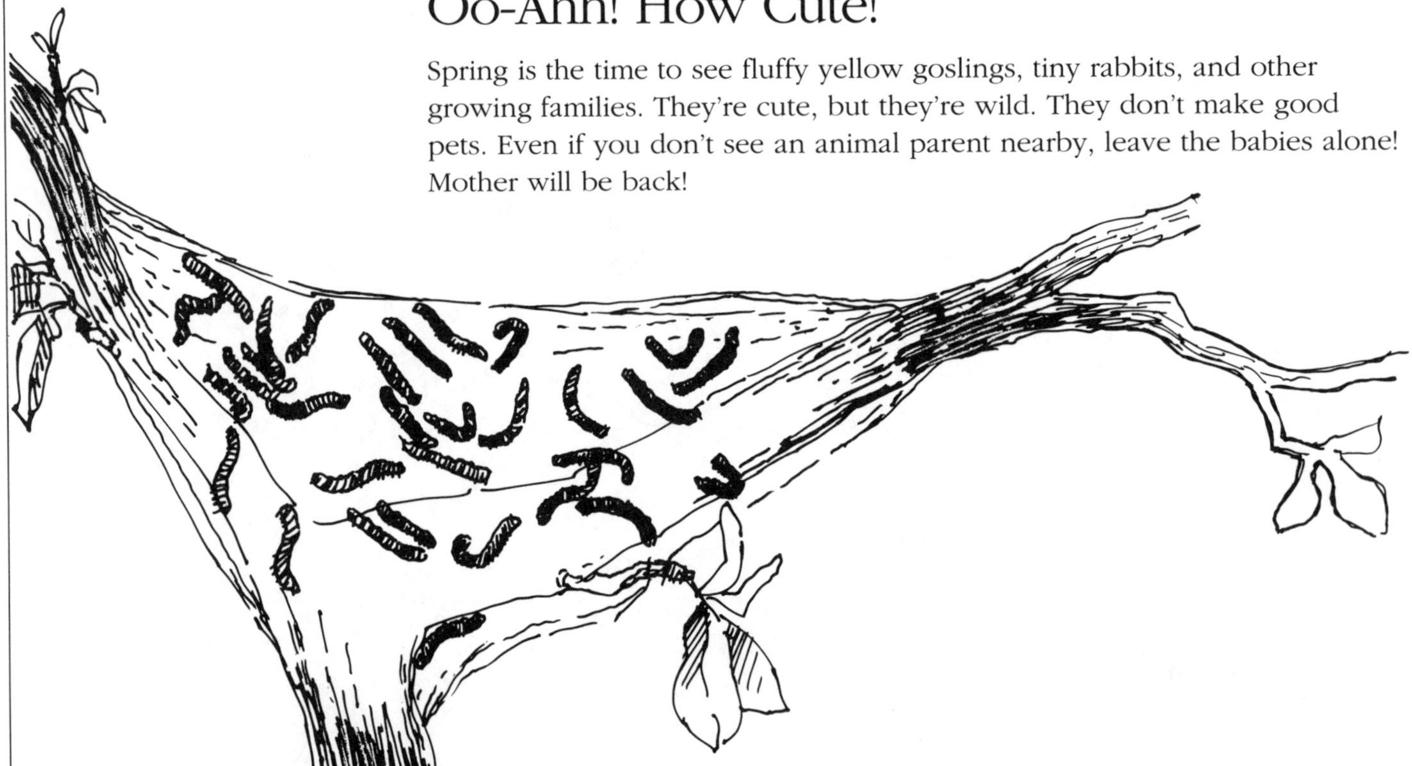

## Lost and Found

**These youngsters have lost their mothers. Can you help?**

| | |
|---|---|
| 1. Gosling | a. Miller moth |
| 2. Pup | b. Spadefoot toad |
| 3. Kitten | c. Mule deer |
| 4. Caterpillar | d. Bluegill |
| 5. Fawn | e. Canada goose |
| 6. Fry | f. Bobcat |
| 7. Cub | g. Prairie dog |
| 8. Tadpole | h. Black bear |

*ANSWERS: 1e, 2g, 3f, 4a, 5c, 6d, 7h, 8b*

## Baby, Look at You Now!

Some animals change so much from young to adult that you might think they were different species.

**Draw lines to link the ones that belong together in this tangle of young and adults.**

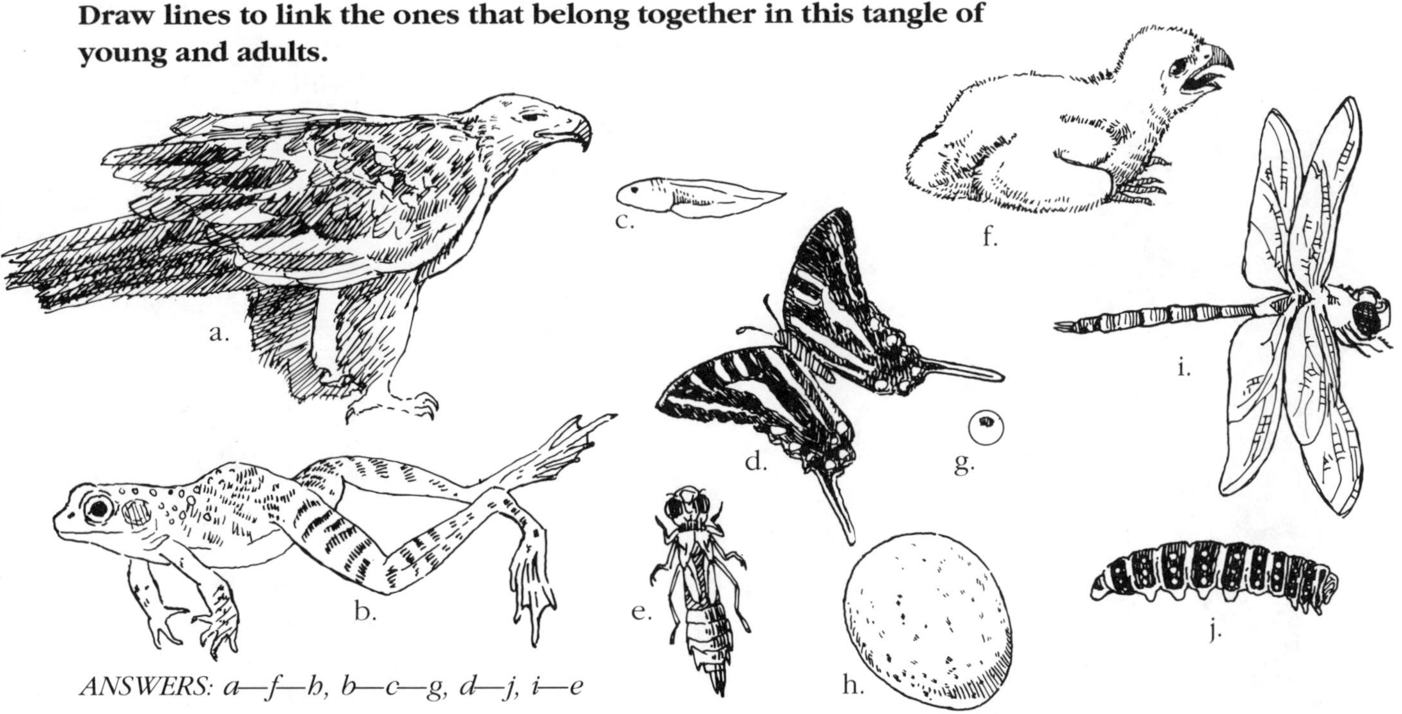


*ANSWERS: a—f—h, b—c—g, d—j, i—e*

# THREATENED AND ENDANGERED

Some animals and plants that used to live in Colorado are extinct. Dinosaurs, saber-toothed cats, and woolly mammoths no longer live here. This situation is natural. Conditions changed over time. These animals could not adapt—so they died out. They became extinct.

Worldwide, animals are becoming extinct at a faster rate now than in the past. More animals are **endangered**. More animals are **threatened**. Here's why:

| | |
|---|---|
| More cities | = Less wild grasslands |
| More highways | = Less continuous habitat |
| More crops for people | = Less varied food for wildlife |
| More wood for building | = Fewer forests for chipmunks |
| More water for lawns | = Less water for fish |
| More poisoning of bugs | = Fewer bugs for birdfood |
| More drained wetlands | = Fewer marshes for frogs |

People may love wildlife. But we still push wildlife out when we want space and need natural resources for ourselves.

We can't do anything about extinct animals. They are gone forever. We *can* do something to prevent more animals and plants from being lost. Threatened and endangered species need our tender, loving care.

Going, going, gone?

Grizzly bear

**Endangered:**
in danger of becoming extinct NOW
**Threatened:**
facing serious survival problems

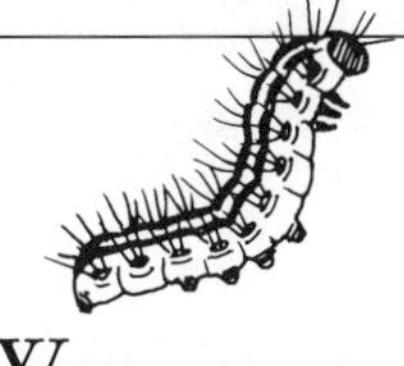

Want to read more about it?
*The Last Bit Bear: A Fable.* Sandra Chisholm Robinson. An endangered species story.
*Wildlife in Danger.* Colorado Division of Wildlife. For Colorado's threatened and endangered animals.

## Too Neat to Lose

**E**=endangered in Colorado **T**=threatened in Colorado

**E** The grizzly bear, a silver-grizzled giant, was last seen in Colorado in 1979.

**E** Black-footed ferrets were one-time predators in prairie dog towns.

**E** Gray wolves are gone from Colorado because they were trapped and poisoned.

**E** River otters are sleek and playful river dwellers. They are being returned to some Colorado wild rivers.

**E** Lynx may still live here—but only tracks have been seen.

**T** Fast swooping peregrine falcons prey on birds.

**E** Bald eagles are our national emblem.

**E** Greater prairie chicken vanish as shortgrass prairie is lost to building and farming.

**T** Greenback cutthroat trout were displaced from cold-water habitats when our rivers were stocked with newcomers—rainbow, brook, and brown trout.

## Why Save Endangered Animals?

*Because they have a right to live*

*Because they have so much to give*

*Because each creature has its role—*

*A tiny part in nature's whole.*

*Because they are too neat to lose.*

*Because we have no right to choose*

*Which ones will die, and which survive.*

*While nature wants them all alive.*

Lynx

A wildlife smile to Denver's peregrine recovery program. Peregrines in high rise "canyons" are great!

## Peregrine Progress

Once peregrines flew wild and free along the Front Range. Diving swiftly to catch birds, they were masters of the air. People used to use a poison called DDT to kill insects. They didn't know DDT stayed poisonous for many years. Small birds ate poisoned bugs. Their bodies contained DDT. Many birds became sick or died. Peregrines caught the small birds and so ate DDT also. The DDT made the peregrine eggs so thin-shelled, they squashed instead of hatching. Whole generations of chicks died. Peregrines became endangered.

DDT is banned now. People are helping peregrines to increase in number. Peregrine chicks are hatched in captivity. When they are old enough to fend for themselves, they are released into a good habitat.

Can you believe that good habitat can be downtown Denver? High buildings are as good as cliffs to a peregrine family. Pigeons make a tasty lunch.

Watch the news to see if Denver's peregrines return each year!

Visit the endangered animals at Denver Zoo (13). Threatened and

# The Last Word

Dinosaurs, ancient mammals, and grasslands teeming with bison are our wildlife past in Colorado.

Beetles, bullfrogs, butterflies, and all the other plants and animals you have seen on your wildwatches are our wildlife present.

What is our wildlife *future*? That depends on you!

■ If you truly care about all wildlife, whether it lives in remote wilderness or shares your city home or yard,

■ if you protect and care for all habitats, large and small,

■ if *enough* people believe this is worth doing (Spread the word!),

. . . then Colorado wildlife will have a good future and there will be wildwatchers still in 20, 50, and 100 years.

Your pledge will complete this book.

I,

______________________________________________,

pledge to help Colorado wildlife by doing these things:

1. ______________________________________________

2. ______________________________________________

3. ______________________________________________

signed: ______________________________________________

date: ______________________________

endangered animals can't be seen easily in the wild!

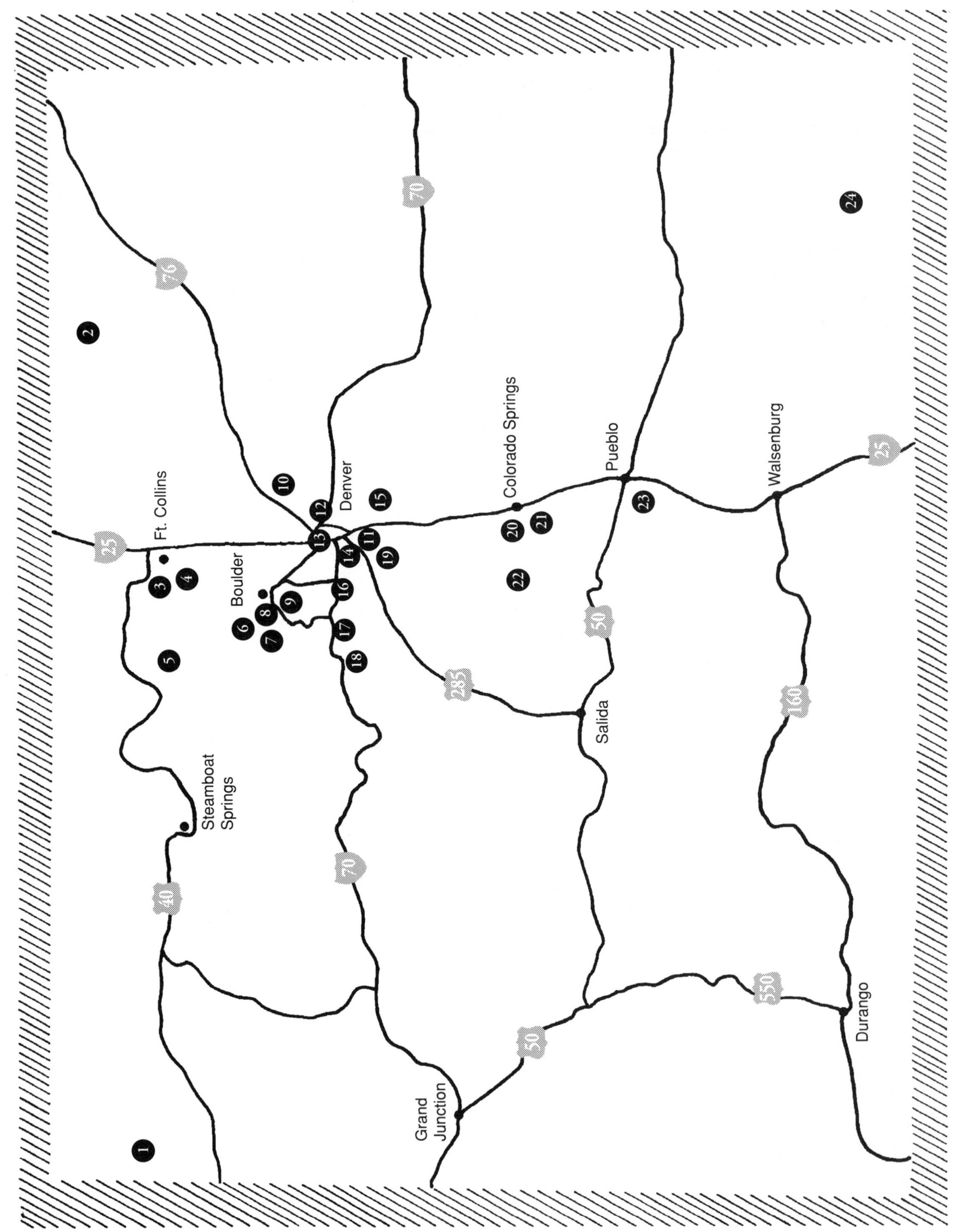
Ft. Collins
Denver
Boulder
Colorado Springs
Pueblo
Walsenburg
Salida
Steamboat Springs
Grand Junction
Durango
25
76
70
40
50
285
160
550
1
2
3
4
5
6
7
8
9
10
11
12
13
14
15
16
17
18
19
20
21
22
23
24

# More About Places to Explore

Here are addresses to find out more about places to explore.

1. **Dinosaur National Monument**
   Dinosaur skeletons and exhibits of diggings
   In northwest Colorado, but well worth the trip.
   *Contact:*
   Dinosaur National Monument, P.O. Box 210, Dinosaur, CO 81610

2. **Pawnee National Grassland**
   Grassland plants and animals
   *Contact:*
   Pawnee National Grasslands, 2009 9th Street, Greeley, CO 80631

3. **City Park of Fort Collins**
   Tree walk
   *Contact:*
   City Forester's Office, 413 South Bryan, Fort Collins, CO 80521

4. **Poudre River Bike Trail**
   River trail and river habitat
   *Contact:*
   Open Space and Trails Department, 413 South Bryan, Fort Collins, CO 80524

5. **Rocky Mountain National Park**
   Bighorn sheep—Horseshoe Park and Specimen Mountain
   Tundra—Trail Ridge Road
   Signs of fire—Ouzel Falls trail
   *Contact:*
   Superintendent, Rocky Mountain National Park, Estes Park, CO 80517

6. **Six-Mile Fold**
   Fossil clams
   *Contact:*
   Boulder County Parks and Open Space Department, P.O. Box 471, Boulder, CO 80306

7. **Boulder Creek**
   River trail and river habitat
   *Contact:*
   Boulder Parks and Recreation Department, P.O. Box 791, Boulder, CO 80306

   **Trout Observatory**
   *Contact:*
   Clarion Harvest House, 1345 28th Street, Boulder, CO 80302

8. **Boulder Mountain Parks**
   Ladybug migration—Green Mountain
   *Contact:*
   Boulder Mountain Parks, P.O. Box 791, Boulder, CO 80306

9. **University of Colorado Museum**
   Insect exhibits
   *Location:*
   Henderson Building, University of Colorado, Boulder, CO 80309

10. **Barr Lake State Park and Nature Center**
    Pond life, wetland birds, and bald eagles
    *Contact:*
    Barr Lake State Park, 13401 Picadilly Road, Brighton, CO 80601

**11. Denver Botanic Gardens**
Butterfly plants
*Location:*
1005 York Street, Denver, CO 80206

**12. Denver Museum of Natural History**
Dinosaurs and prehistoric mammals
Plains Indian life
Colorado habitats
*Location:*
City Park, Denver, CO 80205

**13. Denver Zoo**
Threatened and endangered species
Prairie dogs—Children's Zoo
Animal behavior
*Location:*
City Park, East 23rd Avenue and Steele, Denver, CO 80205

**14. Platte River Greenway System**
River trail with restored river habitat
*Denver section. Contact:*
Platte River Greenway Foundation,
1666 S. University Boulevard
Denver, CO 80110
*Adams County section. Contact:*
Adams County Parks Department,
9755 Henderson Road, Brighton, CO 80601

River trail and wetlands
*Littleton section. Contact:*
South Platte Park,
South Suburban Metropolitan Recreation and Park District,
6315 S. University Boulevard,
Littleton, CO 80121

**15. Plains Conservation Center**
Sod houses and High Plains life
*Location:*
21901 E. Hampden Avenue,
Aurora, CO 80013

**16. Genessee Park**
Bison herd
*Location:*
Off I-70, 20 miles west of Denver, west of El Rancho exit

**17. Mount Evans Highway**
Tundra animals and plants
*Location:*
Off I-70, the Mount Evans exit at Idaho Springs

**18. I-70 at Georgetown**
Bighorn sheep and
other "Watchable Wildlife"
*Contact:*
Colorado Division of Wildlife,
6060 Broadway, Denver, CO 80216

**19. Dinosaur Ridge**
Dinosaur tracks
*Contact:*
Friends of Dinosaur Ridge,
Morrison Natural History Center,
P.O. Box 564, Morrison, CO 80465

**20. Bear Creek Nature Center**
Reptiles, amphibians, and good trails
*Contact:*
Bear Creek Nature Center,
245 Bear Creek Road,
Colorado Springs, CO 80906

**21. Cheyenne Mountain Zoo**

Animal behavior

*Location:*

4250 Cheyenne Mountain Zoo Road,
Colorado Springs, CO 80906

**22. Florissant Fossil Beds National Monument**

Fossil ferns and insects

*Contact:*

Florissant Fossil Beds National Monument,
P.O. Box 185, Florissant, CO 80816

**23. Greenway and Nature Center of Pueblo**

River trail and river habitat

Birds of prey at the Raptor Center

*Location:*

5200 West Nature Center Road,
Pueblo, CO 81003

**24. Comanche Grasslands**

Grassland plants and animals

*Contact:*

Carrizo Ranger District, P.O. Box 127,
Springfield, CO 81070

# Bookworm's Corner


Behler, John L. 1988. *Familiar Reptiles and Amphibians: North America.* The Audubon Society Pocket Guides. Alfred A. Knopf, New York.

Colorado Division of Wildlife. 1986. *Wildlife in Danger.* Colorado Division of Wildlife, Denver, Colorado.

Farrand, John. 1988. *Familiar Insects and Spiders: North America.* The Audubon Society Pocket Guides. Alfred A. Knopf, New York.

Farrand, John. 1988. *Familiar Mammals: North America.* The Audubon Society Pocket Guides. Alfred A. Knopf, New York.

Forey, Pamela. 1988. *An Instant Guide to Insects.* Crown Publishers, Inc., New York.

Halfpenny, James. 1986. *A Field Guide to Mammal Tracking in Western America.* Johnson Books, Boulder, Colorado.

Harrison, Colin. 1978. *A Field Guide to the Nests, Eggs, and Nestlings of North American Birds.* Collins. Cleveland.

Marinos, Nic and Helen. 1981. *Plants of the Alpine Tundra.* Rocky Mountain Nature Association, Inc., Estes Park, Colorado.

National Wildlife Federation. 1986. *Gardening With Wildlife. The Official Backyard Habitat Planning and Planting Kit.* National Wildlife Federation, Washington, D.C.

Opler, Paul A. 1988. *Butterflies of the American West: A Coloring Album.* Roberts Rinehart, Inc., Boulder, Colorado.

Reid, George K. 1967. *A Golden Guide to Pond Life.* Golden Press, New York.

Robertson, Kayo. 1986. *Signs Along the River. Learning to Read the Natural Landscape.* Roberts Rinehart, Inc., Boulder, Colorado.

Robinson, Sandra Chisholm. 1984. *The Last Bit Bear: A Fable.* Roberts Rinehart, Inc., Boulder, Colorado.

Simon, Seymour. 1975. *Pets in a Jar: Collecting and Caring for Small Wild Animals.* Puffin Books. Viking Penguin, Inc., New York.

Tekulsky, Matthew. 1985. *The Butterfly Garden.* The Harvard Common Press, Harvard and Boston, Massachusetts.

Watts, Tom. 1972. *Rocky Mountain Tree Finder.* Nature Study Guild, Berkeley, California.

Zim, Herbert S. and Gabrielson, Ira N. 1956. *Birds. A Guide to the Most Familiar American Birds.* A Golden Nature Guide. Golden Press, New York.

# WILDWORDS

**adaptation**: special feature that an animal or plant is born with that helps it survive in its habitat

**amphibian**: an animal that has two lives—one in water, one on land

**camouflage**: color or shape that helps to conceal

**carnivore**: a meat-eater

**climate**: the average weather of a place

**community**: all the plants and animals that live together in a habitat

**competition**: two kinds of living things trying to use the same resource

**deciduous**: trees that lose all their leaves in winter

**diurnal**: active during the day

**endangered**: in danger of becoming extinct now

**extinct**: none left alive anywhere

**food chain**: the energy pathway from sun to plants to animals

**herbivore**: a plant-eater

**hibernate**: sleep through the winter with the body thermostat turned down—slow heart, slow breathing, slow everything!

**larva**: (more than one is larvae) an early stage in the life of an insect

**metamorphosis**: a change from one form to another

**migrate**: move from one place to another, especially by the seasons

**nocturnal**: active during the night

**omnivore**: an everything-eater

**predator**: an animal that hunts and kills other animals for food

**prehistoric**: a time before events were written down

**prey**: an animal that is hunted and eaten by another animal

**succession**: the changing plants and animals that live in a place as time passes

**territory**: an area defended by an animal to protect a home-site, food, or both of these

**threatened**: facing serious survival problems

**timberline**: the boundary between trees and no trees that climate draws

# INDEX